ONCE WE HAVE FALLEN

Once We Have Fallen

MEGAN E. MORRIS

Mack N' Morris Entertainment

$$\sim 1 \sim$$

"Miss Edwards. Miss Edwards!"

The voice that had barely registered moments before was getting clearer, more insistent now. Angrier too.

I slowly peeled my eyes open, blinking rapidly in the fluorescent glare that greeted me. It took several seconds for my vision to adjust and focus on the room. Where I was seated, and I took quick stock of my surroundings.

The beige paint covering the concrete walls was cracking and had chipped completely away in a few places, revealing ugly gray cinder blocks that contrasted sharply with the brighter color on top. Two dark mauve curtains blocked the only window in the small room, which was lit entirely by the dim light bulbs overhead. Though the window was covered entirely from top to bottom by the ugly purplish drapes, I could see sunlight peeking through the space where the two curtains met each other in the middle. The whiteboard eleven feet in front of me was covered in blue and black writing, mostly dates and names that meant little to me at the moment.

I stared forward at the smear of ink, my mind still in a fog, not fully registering what was happening. Awareness that I was not the only person in the room dawned on me slowly, and I glanced around halfheartedly to look at the other occupants of the enclosure.

Twenty-six pairs of eyes stared back at me. Only twenty-five of those pairs were amused.

Mr. Jenkins, the eleventh made history teacher at Cromwell High School, was not smiling.

"Having a nice nap?" he questioned sarcastically.

The amused faces of my classmates dissolved into tiny chokes of laughter, and I saw several students lift their hands to their mouths in an attempt to hide their growing smiles.

I felt my face grow hot under their gazes as I stared open-mouthed at the teacher standing in front of my desk.

Mr. Jenkins had taught at Cromwell High School in the same position for fifteen years and was notoriously known by every student in the building.

His hair had completely grayed and was thinning slightly in the front. The wrinkles around his eyes and mouth were telling, and I estimated him to be around fifty years old. His age was even more noticeable when compared to the youthful faces of the seventeen-year-old students in the classroom.

Despite his growing years, he was solidly built and displayed no signs of frailty, which benefited him in light of his unpopular standings. The students may have led a mutiny against Mr. Jenkins if he had shown any signs of weakness.

His face, which always displayed a sour expression, was even more acidic than normal as he looked down at me.

By now, my tired brain had rejuvenated enough to give my teacher the response he was looking for.

"I'm sorry," I said quietly, as I tried not to look into his glaring countenance. "I guess I was...I'm sorry," I muttered again.

Katie Henderson, one of the girls in my class, shot me an apologetic look from across the aisle. I smiled weakly at her, then buried my head in my textbook, determined to keep it there for the duration of the class. I could feel the flush slowly leave my cheeks as people returned their attention to Mr. Jenkins, who was now back at the front of the classroom.

The lesson resumed, Mr. Jenkins voice droning on monotonously, and I wished for the hundredth time that I lived somewhere, anywhere else. It seemed that every day I was finding some new and inventive way to embarrass myself, and in a town as small as West Liberty, it was hard to hide my many humiliations.

I reflected on some of my more degrading episodes, burrowing my head deeper into the book in front of me as if it could shield me from the past. We had only lived here a year, but the entire town already knew I was a klutz.

Thankfully the bell rang, sparing me any more reflection on my own ungainliness. I packed up my book bag and tried to make my way out of the classroom without tripping over any desks or backpacks, which were strewn about the aisle.

As I walked through the hallway, I thought again about the day my family had relocated to West Liberty. My father and mother had insisted that the move from the bustling metropolis of Orlando, Florida to the tranquil atmosphere and rolling hills of West Liberty, West Virginia would be a welcome and relaxing change for both my brother and me. No more smog filled skies, overcrowded housing developments, or exorbitant crime rates they promised.

They were certainly right about that, and I had to admit that the peaceful atmosphere was much more agreeable to me than the hectic city life of Orlando.

As we drove into town that first day, the sight that greeted us was drastically different than what I was used to.

Orlando had always been bustling, with stores for any and every need. It was considered commonplace to have multiple food venues, clothing departments, and restaurants all contained within a single city block.

Downtown West Liberty consisted of a small bowling alley, a rundown movie theatre, a single pizza joint, a coffeehouse that doubled as a restaurant, an ice cream parlor, a small pharmacy, a grocery store, and two gas stations bordering the northern edge of town. There were also several churches dotted throughout the community and surrounding countryside.

Housing in the city had been tight, with buildings squeezed one beside the other for miles on end. Here, the mountainous landscape stretched indefinitely, and post-civil war manors, now fully restored, lay on sprawling estates outside the township. The old-world architecture and expanses of open land only added to the quaint feel West Liberty exuded.

The population here bordered the two thousand mark and the high school consisted of only two hundred and fifty-eight students. Everybody knew everybody else in town by name. Nothing remained a secret for long, and every resident was well informed about the comings and goings in the small town.

Though we were aware that West Liberty was a close-knit community, it was still a surprise when half the town showed up on our front lawn the first day welcoming us to the area. Apparently, our impending arrival had been talked about for weeks prior to the move.

Most residents of the small town had greeted my parents by name, and it didn't take long before everyone knew my younger brother's and mine as well.

The first day of sophomore year in my new school had been full of welcoming smiles and pleasant introductions, but that hadn't been enough to ease my discomfort at being the center of attention. I felt like I was on display, with a label attached to my clothes that screamed I'm the new girl. It seemed that wherever

I went, there was always a group of people watching me, and if I turned my head fast enough, I would occasionally catch their stares before they had time to avert their eyes.

Being the center of interest did not suit me for a number of reasons, the main one being that the attention only seemed to usher on my embarrassing moments and consequently red cheeks.

That was the real reason I wished I were somewhere else most of the time. It was easier to blend in and be ignored in a large crowd, and I often found myself longing for the anonymity offered by the big city. Here, there was nowhere to hide.

My parents hadn't understood my uneasiness. They always insisted that I was a beautiful, smart girl with a wonderful personality, and had no reason to be uncomfortable here.

They were right about one thing at least. I somehow was at the top of my class academically at Cromwell, having never brought home anything less than an A on a report card.

The rest of their conclusions were certainly open to interpretation. I didn't consider stammering over every phrase to be a great social trait, and my looks were surely only average. Like most teenage girls, I had often stared at my own reflection in the mirror trying to see myself as others might upon first glance. Five-foot five, average build, dark brown hair that hung in waves just past my shoulder blades, light brown eyes with just a hint of green on the inner edge, and a smooth, naturally tan complexion. Nothing like the statuesque models with porcelain skin splayed across fashion magazines.

Despite my mildly shy disposition, I had eventually settled in with a small group of friends who were kind enough to overlook my frequently embarrassing public displays of clumsiness.

I sighed as I reached my locker, and absently began spinning the combination lock on the handle.

"Callee!" The sound of my name being spoken broke me out of my trancelike state. I turned my head to see Nathan, one of my closest friends, waving and winding his way through the hall in my direction. I couldn't help but smile and wave back.

Nathan had been one of the first people to acknowledge me on that day almost a year ago. I was sitting in my first-period class and our teacher had just begun the lesson for the day. I had opened my notebook and was reaching into my backpack for a pen, coming up empty-handed after a thorough search. Nathan was sitting across the aisle from me and seemed to notice my dilemma. He had dug around in his bookbag for a minute before wordlessly offering me a pencil. I smiled at him, grateful that he had saved me from being the absentminded new girl who didn't even remember to bring a writing utensil on her first day of school. Ever since that day Nathan had always been there for me.

We headed for the front door of Cromwell, weaving in and out around students still loitering in the building. Outside, more students awaited buses or milled around their cars talking to classmates. A few waved in our direction as Nathan and I began walking towards our houses. It had been our tradition since day one to walk home from school together since we only lived three houses apart from each other.

"You ready for the Homecoming dance tomorrow night?" Nathan asked amicably as we passed the pizzeria on Main Street.

I felt a frown touch my lips. "You mean that torture of spinning in circles on impossibly small heels, while simultaneously trying not to fall on your face or injure your partner's unsuspecting toes? Not to mention being graceful while doing all this. Ready as I'll ever be," I responded wryly.

This drew another chuckle from Nathan. "Some people call that fun you know."

"Sick, aren't they," I thought aloud.

Truthfully, I enjoyed the part where I got to dress up and look like royalty for the night. It was a rare occurrence that allotted this privilege in West Liberty.

"At least I don't have to worry about having my parents meet my date," I continued as Nathan and I turned the corner onto Westbrook Drive.

I am glad everyone decided to go as a group this year. It spared me one intense humiliation at least. I couldn't imagine the interrogation any boy other than a friend would get if they came walking through my front door.

"You know it wouldn't be that bad," Nathan offered encouragingly. "I mean, they like me." He grinned l devilishly at this thought and I found myself smiling at his humor.

He was right about that. My parents loved him. They often suggested that Nathan and I go on a date, which was usually followed by my immediate blush and some mumbled excuse as I left the room.

It's not that the thought of dating Nathan totally disgusted me, but I certainly didn't feel anything beyond friendship for my closest companion.

I often got the impression that Nathan did not feel the same detachment I did, but so far he hadn't made any move to betray his real emotions, and I certainly wasn't going to push the matter.

To tell the truth, I often hoped he would never confess anything other than camaraderie to me. It would certainly complicate things if I had to tell him I didn't like him in return, and I never wanted to risk damaging our friendship. We continued to chat idly about our plans for tomorrow as we walked.

Everybody was meeting at my house at six in the evening and from there, we were going to split up into two cars and drive thirty minutes to Wheeling for supper before returning for the main event. The dance wouldn't start until eight and was held in the high school gym every year.

Nathan waved goodbye as he went up the sidewalk to his home. I stopped and returned his farewell before continuing towards my own house.

I had barely taken five steps when the distinct sounds of running behind me made me stop again, and I turned to see who was following me

Jaden, my brother, was smiling as he closed the space between us. Though only a fourth-grader, he was surprisingly quick, and it didn't take long for him to catch up to where I stood.

He looked so much like me that nobody could mistake us for anything but brother and sister. The only thing that separated us from one another was the color of our eyes. While I had inherited my dad's brown eyes, Jaden had gotten mom's green ones.

Those deep green eyes were excited now, as Jaden told me about his day at school and proudly showed off his latest art project. His enthusiasm was always contagious and I found myself smiling as we walked the short distance to our house.

I stopped outside our residence to admire the place for a minute. It was a two-story ranch-style house, updated recently with a light grayish-blue siding and white trim around all the windows.

In Orlando, we had lived in a small apartment in the city. While the location was convenient for our parents' early morning work commute, it had left little in the way of personal space. Jaden and I had shared a bedroom up until our move to West Liberty.

At least here we each had our own bedroom in addition to two bathrooms, which made morning showers easier to come by.

The insistent tug on my hand reminded me that my nine-year-old brother was impatient to get in the house and relive his day for our parents. We continued up the walkway and through the front door.

I could see my mom in the kitchen as I stepped onto the mottled brown living room carpet. Jaden's book bag hit the floor with a thud as he tore through the house in search of our Labrador puppy, Boz.

I settled on a more relaxing pace as I made my way into the sunlit kitchen.

"Hi Mom," I threw over my shoulder as I made my way to the refrigerator to grab a snack.

"Oh, hi honey," she said happily, turning away from the sink to focus her attention on me.

My mom had always been pretty with her green eyes and champagne blonde hair, and the light streaming in through the kitchen windows only highlighted her good looks.

"How was school today?" she asked as she leaned on the island in the middle of the room.

I pulled a yogurt out of the fridge, grabbing a spoon before sitting on a barstool across the counter from her.

"It wasn't too horrifying today, although I did get caught sleeping in history class," I answered with a grimace. Just thinking about it made me flush again.

My parents were never particularly strict, not that I had ever warranted their sternness, but I caught the disapproving gaze my mother gave me just then. I
swallowed what was in my mouth.

"I swear it's the first time I have ever fallen asleep in class. I was just really tired today," I promised her.

"Not sleeping well?" she prodded, her displeasure changing instantly to maternal concern.

Though it was hardly an inquisition, I could feel myself searching for an excuse to give her for my recent lack of sleep. I couldn't tell her about the dreams that were keeping me up every night.

No, definitely could not tell her about those.

"I don't know," I offered in an attempt to avoid her question. "I guess I just need to get to bed a bit earlier." I shoved another spoonful of yogurt into my mouth, hoping this last sentence would placate her.

She eyed me for a few minutes, finally deciding it wasn't much to worry over, before turning back to the sink to finish washing the vegetables on the sideboard.

My mind reverted to the dream that had been haunting me every night for the past few weeks.

In it, I was floating over West Liberty, just watching the town and its occupants as they idled along. It was almost like I was waiting for something to happen. I'm not sure what that something was, but the feeling was there nonetheless.

Within the past week, the dream had shifted, a new element added from the nights preceding. Where before I had been alone during my flight, now l had the distinct impression that something else was there floating along with me. Although the presence never quite materialized itself, I could sense its existence, also keeping watch on the sleepy village.

I shook my head to clear the memory.

While nothing bad ever happened in these dreams, they were still unnerving and were enough to wake me several times a night with a start. I almost expected to see somebody sitting in the corner of my room watching me, but the place was always empty.

I needed to distract myself from this train of thought.

"Need any help with supper mom," I offered. She smiled, sliding a cutting board with some washed vegetables on it towards me and handing me a knife. I gladly seized the opportunity to do something besides dwell on my nightly visions.

"Are you ready for the big dance?" my mom questioned. I could feel a potential inquest coming on and tried to pacify her need for knowledge.

"I guess so. I have had the dress for weeks and am looking forward to getting out of West Liberty for a few hours."

I could see her smile out of the corner of my eye and knew exactly what was coming next.

"Are you and Nathan going together?"

"No Mom," I said, willing myself not to blush. "All of us are going as a group."

She continued with other questions about the Homecoming dance. What time were we meeting, who was going, where we were going, and what time would I be home tomorrow night. I answered her as best I could trying to keep up with the frenzied pace of her thoughts.

"What are your plans for tonight?" she asked.

"Well, the homecoming game is this evening, so I think I will probably go to that. I need to get my homework done too. I know the rest of the weekend will be too busy to think about it."

Jaden and Boz picked that moment to come bounding into the kitchen. The focus of my mom's attention shifted from me to my little brother, and I grasped the opportunity to slip away from the kitchen and my mom's never-ending questions. I headed upstairs, picking my backpack up on my way past the front hall and taking it with me to my room. *Might as well start on my homework while I have the chance*, I thought.

The rest of the night passed uneventfully. I ate supper with my family as usual then headed upstairs to get ready for the football game.

It was only September, but already the nighttime chill was hinting that a cool fall was in store just around the corner.

As I adjusted my black and gold Cromwell Falcons sweatshirt, my mind drifted back to the dream.

Maybe tonight will be different, I thought.

I grabbed a pair of gloves and said goodbye to my parents before headed out the front door. The gust of cool evening air and the twilight skyline erased all thoughts of the dream from my head as I set out for the football stadium.

~ 2 ~

I was flying.

There was nothing holding me up, nothing holding me back. I was free.

The town of West Liberty was beneath me, and I gazed at it with intense interest. I could see people, barely more than a speck of color against the pavement, going about the daily routine, unaware they were being watched from above. Cars were winding down roadways, carving a path through the town, into the country, and beyond. Clusters of trees speckled the scenic landscape, and I could hear the faint rustling of leaves in the early morning breeze and smell their woodsy scent in the air. Groups of houses in town gave way to scattered country homes and large, grandiose manors as I looked about the surrounding countryside.

Shoppers, students, houses, woods, nothing was hidden from my eyes.

Despite the time and the gusts of wind, I wasn't cold. Rather, I welcomed the freshness of the day surrounding me, reveling in the beautiful scenery spread before my eyes.

I sensed the presence beside me once again. Not intrusive, but still there. It was watching.

I turned my head, expecting to see nothing as usual, but was surprised to spot a person's figure floating a few feet away from my own. Somehow the presence had taken shape and was no longer an It at all, but a human person.

Not just a person, I realized with a start, but a boy. He could not be much older than me as he was about the same size and build as most of the guys in my class. His body was lean at the waist but tapered outwardly as my gaze traveled upward, showing broad, muscular shoulders. He was tall too, probably close to six feet.

The white linen-draped around his frame flapped in the breeze. It was almost blinding in its intensity, brighter than any white I had ever laid eyes on.

I tried to catch a glimpse of his face as he floated in and out of the beams of sunlight breaking through the clouds. I focused my vision, squinting my eyes to capture any detail that I could, but no matter how hard I strained, I could not seem to get a good look at him.

"Callee." His voice took me by surprise. Velvety smooth, making my name sound angelic as it came off his lips. How did he know my name?

I sensed a smile on his lips as he repeated my name again. "Callee."

"Callee. Calleeeee, wake up." Not the same smooth voice from before.

I peeked out from under my eyelids and came face to face with Jaden's worried green eyes. "Callee, are you okay?"

Jaden could not keep the concern from showing in his voice.

I sat up, staring at the rain softly beating on the glass pane of my bedroom window, its steady tapping bringing me fully awake.

I had been dreaming again. It was just a dream.

I turned and looked into Jaden's eyes, suddenly remembering that he was standing there waiting for me to answer him. "I'm fine," I said breathlessly.

Jaden continued to watch me carefully.

"You were talking in your sleep," he stated, still taking in my disheveled appearance.

"I was?"

I had never been known to talk in my sleep before. The vision had felt so real though. I could still see the scenery beneath me and feel the wind rushing past my face. I could still *sense him.*

I tried to calm my panting breaths enough to ease Jaden's fears. "I'm fine," I said again. His look told me he didn't believe me yet. To confirm my statement, I stretched my cramped muscles and stood up. "What time is it, squirt."

His worried face broke as a grin spread across his lips. "It's almost ten o'clock. Mom told me to come get you up for breakfast sleepyhead."

I had always been more of a night owl than an early bird, so I guess I wasn't too surprised that I had slept in a little late. In addition, I hadn't gotten a decent night's rest over the past few weeks. My tired body was definitely trying to catch up on what it had missed.

I trudged into the bathroom, preparing to go about my usual morning routine.

The person from my dream seemed to accompany my thoughts as I showered and got ready to face the day. Who was he? Somebody I knew? Why was he there, in my dream?

The questions swirled around in my head without an answer.

When I was decent enough for human company, I joined my family downstairs for breakfast. I could hear the rain continue to assault the house as I poured myself a bowl of cereal in the kitchen.

I reached the living room and was halfway through my bowl of cereal before remembering that today was the Homecoming Dance. Only a few measly hours stood between intense humiliation and my sanity.

I spent the morning relaxing, mentally preparing myself for the night that lay before me.

At noon, the girls started arriving at my house. In Orlando, mom had been a hairdresser and had promised my girlfriends that she would do all our hair and makeup for the big event free of charge. It seemed my entire circle of girlfriends had accepted the offer, and were now crowded into the living room of our house, waiting their turn while talking excitedly about the night ahead.

The enthusiasm in the room eventually caught up to me and I found myself feeling a little better about the dance than I had earlier that morning.

Jackie Diller, a beautiful blond with clear blue eyes, had been one of the first to arrive.

Of all the girls in my circle of friends, Jackie was definitely. She had befriended me shortly after the move and was one of the sincerest people in West Liberty. Her personality was kind but energizing, and everybody naturally gravitated towards her. She was quick to give a compliment, laugh at a joke, or smile at a newcomer. Jackie was easily the most beautiful girl, both inside and out, in West Liberty, and I was truly happy to count her a friend.

Next to show up had been Amber, Rachel, and Kathryn. They laughed as the wind and rain blew them soaking wet through our front door, and had promptly engulfed me in a tight, albeit drenching, hug.

I smiled in spite of myself. It was nice to have such a group of friends surrounding me.

It was amazing to see the transformation that took place in my house. Each girl went into the kitchen looking like a normal sixteen-year-old, and came out more grown-up and elegant, with hair piled up in riotous curls and secured in bobby pins at the top of their head. My mom had truly been given a talent, and I was grateful to her for her help.

My turn came, and I sat upright in the chair as my own transformation took place. Instead of pinning my hair up, my mom left my long hair down and curled it so that it hung in elegant spirals, ending just between my shoulder blades. She added a sprinkling of sparkles to complete the look. Next, she started in on my makeup, her sure brushstrokes quickly completing the task. As the final touches were added, she handed me a mirror so I could inspect her work.

I gasped at the image before me. My eyes looked large and luminous in the kitchen light. The faint red tinge on my cheeks and lips looked alluring but natural as if I had been in the sun for just a few minutes too long.

"You look, gorgeous honey," Mom assured me, delighted at my reaction. I smiled and thanked her profusely, walking from the kitchen back into the living room, where the girls gushed over my new look.

By now, it was five thirty, so we all headed upstairs to change into our dresses. The array of colors was dazzling. Jackie had picked a blue dress which perfectly offset her eyes. Amber had chosen a for fitting gold dress that shimmered from head to toe as she walked underneath the light, while Rachel had opted for a red halter dress that ended mid-calf. Kathryn looked stunning in a spaghetti strap green mermaid dress and matching high heels. I gazed at her feet in agony as I again thought about navigating a crowded gym on those shoes that faintly resembled circus stilts.

My own dress was an off-white halter which fell all the way to the floor and matching off-white heels. The top of the dress was fitted to my ribcage, while the bottom of the dress flared out in an A-frame starting at the waist. I twirled in front of the mirror feeling like a movie star.

Below we heard the doorbell ring signaling the boys' arrival. I took one last look in the mirror before walking, well, tripping down the steps.

The boys looked good in their black suits and ties with white dress shirts underneath. They were fidgeting uncomfortably as we emerged in the living room. People hugged and gave compliments, smiling at the night to come. Most of our parents were there also, snapping pictures and making everyone pose for the camera. My mom forced Nathan and me into a photo of just the two of us. I was too embarrassed to say anything, but Nathan smiled graciously and struck a pose with me.

We finally convinced them that we needed to get going in order to make it in time for our dinner reservations. The boys were thoughtful enough to bring umbrellas, and we walked animatedly out to the cars parked in the driveway.

"Hey there beautiful," Nathan greeted me, smiling. I felt myself blush and smile in return.

"Thanks. I feel graceful tonight for a change." It was true. Despite the torture devices on my feet, I was somehow managing to keep my balance as we made our way down the slippery walk.

Nathan took my hand and kissed it before holding open the car door for me. I hoped the makeup was hind the red that crept into my cheeks.

We had ten people altogether, so both cars were packed to the max as we drove into Wheeling.

Dinner was lighthearted and fun. We had all agreed to go to an Italian restaurant on the edge of town. We weren't the only students from Cromwell in the restaurant, but we were certainly the largest group. The waiters had to push several tables together in order to accommodate us.

Nathan had taken the seat on my right and Jackie was seated on my left. I was happy to find that I was actually enjoying myself so far.

After dinner, we piled into the ems and drove back into West Liberty. It seemed like most people had paired off into couples while at dinner, and I naturally, but to my growing chagrin, I had been paired up with Nathan for the evening. I tried to relax and smile like normal.

We arrived at the school at around eight-thirty amidst a throng of other Cromwell students. Everybody bought tickets at the front table before passing through to the gym.

As we walked into the gymnasium, there was an audible intake of breath as all ten of us stopped to admire the handiwork of the student council.

The theme for the night was "Captured in a Dream," and the gym seemed to reflect the very essence of a dreamlike state. Smoke curled at our feet, creating a haze that was ethereal. A fake moon and hundreds of glittering stars had been suspended from the ceiling. Even the walls were covered in silver tinsel, which reflected any light it caught and sparkled in the din of the room.

We made our way toward an arch decorated with silver balloons, which had been put up as a background for picture taking. What followed were several group photos, including one with just the girls together and one with just the guys together. I even consented to another picture of Nathan and I alone, though we lightened the serious mood by making faces at the camera instead of a traditional couple pose.

Several tables had been set up on the outskirts of the gym, and our group commandeered one on which we set all our purses, coats, and cameras.

In the blink of an eye, I found myself being pulled out onto the dance floor. For the next hour straight, I found myself spinning in a whirlwind of lights, colors, and sounds as upbeat music blared out of the DJ's speaker system. Several of the guys shed their suit jackets and ties, as the air became hot and stifling in the small room, and the girls opted for bare feet in lieu of the torturous heels.

It wasn't until halfway through the evening that disaster finally struck.

I had been doing fairly well so far, considering my track record of unfortunate and embarrassing events. The tempo had slowed down several times throughout the night, and I had accepted slow dances from the guys who asked. I had even managed to not crush a single toe yet. When the beat again slowed, Nathan pulled me onto the dance floor insisting I owed him at least one dance.

"Are you having fun," he asked cheerfully, as I wrapped my arms around his neck and he placed his on my waist.

"This may surprise you," I answered, looking at my bare feet, "but I am having a good time."

He was quiet for several minutes as we swayed and turned to the music. Then he cleared his throat.

"Listen, Cal, I have something I really want to talk to you about."

I sensed his somber mood and looked up into his face. What I saw there shocked me. His blue eyes were soft and his normally smiling face was serious. I quickly looked down again.

No, no, no my mind cried quietly. I don't want this to happen. Our friendship was special and important to me, and I did not want anything to change.

Hadn't I guessed this moment would come through? I silently cursed myself for not preparing a response to this situation ahead of time. I had known and had chosen to do nothing, simply hoping for the best. Now it was too late. There was no time to rehearse an answer that would keep our friendship securely intact, and I was sure to say something that would only cause great sadness.

My steps faltered and my feet snared the hem of my dress. It wasn't long before my lower limbs were completely entangled in my full skirt. I lost my balance and felt my world tilt dangerously. I was falling, right there in the middle of the dance floor. I had prepared myself for the impact of flesh and bone against hardwood, closing my eyes expectantly, but there was nothing.

Great, just great, I thought inwardly. I hit my head on the gym floor and passed out in front of everybody. Callee strikes again.

It took several seconds before I realized the soft hands that supported my back. I opened my eyes. Though the dance floor had cleared around me, nobody was staring in horror, which was a fairly good sign I hadn't been seriously injured. I even saw Nathan still standing upright next to me.

It was then I looked into the eyes of the person crouching beside me, hands still on my back. I felt my jaw drop slightly. Maybe I had passed out after all.

Gray eyes, the color of the Atlantic on a winter day, stared down at me. His face, though etched with worry, was perfect in every sense of the word. I took in his squared jaw, straight nose, and fair skin. No flaw marred his complexion. I realized I was staring and tried to avert my gaze, but I couldn't pull my eyes away from that beautiful face. His dark blonde hair shone in the dim light, and the muscles under his white shirt flexed as he laid me gently on the floor.

"Are you okay," he asked, his voice so mellow and smooth it sounded like liquid honey. I stared at his mouth, liking the way his full lips moved as they formed the words.

"Callee?" It was Nathan's voice that now spoke to me. I glanced away from the stranger as Nathan kneeled on the floor and took my hand in his.

I found my voice then. "I'm fine," I said quickly, glancing from one concerned face to the other.

Was I really? I did a quick mental scan of my body and found that my ankle was throbbing a little. "I may have twisted my ankle though," I admitted sheepishly. I looked pointedly at the stranger again. He smiled then, showing off his perfectly straight, blindingly white teeth.

"Perhaps we should get her off the floor," he suggested to Nathan calmly, taking his eyes from me for the first time.

Nathan looked at the stranger then too, nodding his head in agreement. The boys each took an arm and hauled me off the floor back onto my one good foot. They both helped support my weight as I hobbled to sit at our table on the sidelines.

~ 3 ~

After we were seated, I rubbed my ankle, happy to note that the pain was quickly receding. There was no swelling either. It looked like I would live to dance another day. I cringed inwardly at this thought. Maybe I should consider early retirement from the world of dance instead.

No longer concerned about my ankle, I turned my attention back to the gorgeous creature sitting beside me.

I took a moment to study the stranger in my peripheral vision. Like most of the guys present, he was dressed in black pants and a white starched shirt, both of which seemed perfectly tailored to his body. There was something else though. Something that had nothing to do with the way he was dressed. At first glance, I had just thought his skin incredibly fair. Looking at him now, it almost seemed that he was glowing, not like a lightning bug, flashing or eye-catching, but more like a pale peach light emanating from just beneath the surface of his skin. It sounded crazy, but the more I looked, the more my assessment seemed true.

Given his height, I guessed him to be my age, but maybe even slightly older. He was obviously still in High School if he was attending a Homecoming Dance.

As if sensing my scrutiny, he turned and caught my gaze. I looked into those gray eyes again, lost for a moment in their depth and intensity.

"I suppose I should thank you for saving my head from certain concussion," I remarked after regaining my senses. I suddenly realized that this compelling person had obviously seen my display of gracelessness on the dance floor, and I blushed furiously. It bothered me that he might believe me a klutz like everybody else.

His lips parted, and that mesmerizing voice once again spoke. "It was my pleasure."

Those four simple words were sending chills all over my body, running the length of my skin and back again.

"I'm so sorry Cal," Nathan apologized from my other side. I turned to look at him. His face was so earnest and sincere. "I should have caught you, but you fell so fast I just didn't have time to react."

"No harm done," I insisted, giving him a smile in an attempt to assuage any guilt he may feel. It really wasn't his fault that I tripped all over myself the moment I was slightly upset.

"I should also offer my thanks," Nathan said, now directing his gaze at my rescuer. It seemed he was sizing up our newcomer. Apparently not sensing any danger there, Nathan pushed on. "I didn't even see you nearby before Callee fell. One minute we were along, and the next you were beside us." It wasn't really a question, but Nathan was still trying to find an explanation for the sudden appearance.

"I was watching the dancing from across the room," the stranger replied smoothly. The idea that he may have been watching me sent another wave of trembling along my spine. "I noticed her trip and could see her feet getting tangled in her dress. It was inevitable that she would fall," he continued.

"I know I have never seen you at Cromwell before. What is your name'? Where are you from?" Nathan questioned politely.

I could have kissed Nathan right then. I certainly wanted to know more about this mysterious outsider with gray eyes, and Nathan was unknowingly placating my curiosity.

The stranger furrowed his brow and did not answer right away, which seemed odd to me. The question was quite direct, the kind of thing people ask you all the time. Maybe he is nervous I mused, smiling encouragingly just in case. It was funny to imagine this stranger slightly flustered by our presence.

After what seemed like several minutes he finally answered. "My name is Ian Evans. I'm not from anywhere nearby. I am just in town for a few days visiting an acquaintance."

While his answer seemed polite enough, I could not help but think he was hiding or withholding something. In my head I chastised my pessimistic reaction. If he did not want to share certain aspects of his visit to West Liberty, he was certainly within his rights to omit the information, and I should not press him if he was purposefully leaving some unknown reason out.

"My name is Nathan. This graceful beauty beside me is Callee," Nathan added with a smile. So like Nathan, politely welcoming the stranger with his openness.

"And how long will you be staying in town Ian?" I asked, trying desperately to hide my mowing interest as well as my reddened cheeks.

Again, it seemed he stopped to ponder the question. "I'm not really sure, but I imagine for a few weeks at least. I could very well be here for several months."

Once again, I reminded myself not to pry too much into his personal life. "Does that mean you will be attending Cromwell? If you will be here a while, you certainly don't want to fall behind in your education."

His eyes looked directly at mine. "I am looking into that currently," he stated.

I couldn't help but feel the excitement and intrigue rise up inside me as his eyes stayed upon my face. It would certainly be nice if he could stay in West Liberty for several months. For some inexplicable reason, I felt drawn to him, not only physically, but mentally as well. I needed time to get to know him better, time to find out more about him.

"Are you sure you are okay," Nathan asked me again, mistaking my sudden silence for pain. "Should I take you home?"

"I promise I am fine. Actually, my ankle doesn't hurt at all anymore." I tried not to look at Nathan as I gave this answer, hoping he could not hear the deception in my voice. While it was true my ankle did not hurt, I did not divulge my other motive for wanting to stay. That unspoken reason was now staring at me unabashedly with his intense gray eyes. It was a full minute before I realized I was holding my breath.

I gulped down a lungful of air, the sudden intake causing a slight burn in my lungs. After taking a few more deep breaths, I felt steadier, and my mind began to work overtime, looking for some excuse to talk to this stranger privately.

The music, which had been quick moments before, slowed again, creating an almost perfect opportunity. "At the very least, I owe my rescuer a dance," I stated with a shy smile.

"If you dare sir," Nathan offered with a whoop. While I could have shaken him for his usual joking comment in front of Ian, I tried to maintain calm, both inside and out.

Ian just smiled, seeming to find Nathan's warning unwarranted, as he stood up and offered me his outstretched hand. I took it, noticing the immediate warmth his skin let off. Somehow, the innocent contact felt charged with energy, yet natural at the same time. We walked quietly onto the dance floor. I wrapped one arm around Ian's neck and he placed one hand on my waist. My other hand he enfolded in his own, tucking both neatly against his chest. It felt both comforting and personal as it rested there.

"So Callee, tell me something about yourself?"

The way he said my name made every bone in my body liquefy instantly. I certainly would have been on the floor again if not for Ian's strong arms supporting me.

He looked at me expectantly. I tried hard to focus on his question, but my mind was a complete blank. I wracked my brain, but suddenly, nothing I could say felt the least bit interesting. After a bit of thought, I settled on a safe topic.

"My family and I just moved here a year ago from Orlando, Florida." Good so far. At least Ian was pretending to be interested. "We live in a house on Westbrook Drive," I continued. "I have only one younger brother, Jaden. He's nine and highly incorrigible." I added this last phrase, thinking about my imp of a sibling, and I knew I was smiling despite the words I had spoken. Jaden and I had always been close despite our age difference. While most of my friends argued with their younger brothers, I found that Jaden offered me warmth and an exciting way of viewing everyday life. Everything he did was a new adventure to him, and he couldn't help but spread his excitement with anyone who would listen. His teachers were always gushing about how bright and unique he was to have in class, and I couldn't help but feel a little sisterly pride every time somebody said that.

Something about my face must have touched Ian deeply because his own expression softened as he looked at me. "What about you'? Do you have any brothers or sisters?" I asked.

"No."

His quick answer surprised me. I couldn't explain the emotion that crossed his face just then, but it made me feel sad, and my heart went out to Ian.

"Are you okay?" I asked softly.

He looked a little surprised at my question, taking in my face as I asked it again. It was almost as if he didn't believe I could see the hurt clearly shown in his eyes. We continued swaying to the music, but my look never left his face, and his never left mine.

His every attitude was captivating. It seemed like every expression — happiness, sadness, hurt, fear –was unique to him. I liked that every emotion he had flitted across his steel-gray eyes, giving away his thoughts before he had a chance to mask them.

After several moments of charged silence, an easy grin touched his features. "I'm really okay. Sony, my mind is a hundred miles away right now. Please forgive me."

Forgiveness was certainly easy to offer this handsome new arrival. I smiled. "You're forgiven."

His hand found my cheek and his eyes, soft and enchanting, looked at me in silent appraisal. For a moment, my wild imagination took flight. I leaned into his hand, pressing my cheek into the warmth there and closing my eyes contentedly. The room around me dimmed, as if the world had suddenly narrowed to only include Ian and myself. We continued swaying to the music, my feet feeling light and graceful beneath me. I leaned in a few more inches, noticing the musky smell that clung to his skin. I looked back up, drinking in his remarkable features. If only he would lean down a few more inches... That thought, though fleeting, suddenly seemed to take on reality, as Ian's head bent closer to mine. I parted my lips in anticipation.

The tempo of the music changed again, picking back up and throwing off the enchantment that cloaked the moment. Ian shuddered with a start and dropped his hand from my cheek, as if the contact had burned him like a hot iron. He took two steps away from me and straightened his shoulders. The moment was broken and whatever spell had been cast had now fallen from around us. His eyes again took on a distant look as he took my hand and guided me back to the sideline, where Nathan sat with an angry, tormented look on his face. I had completely forgotten he was watching, and I could feel the color creep to my face, embarrassed he had witnessed the moment on the dance floor.

"Nathan, I truly appreciate your kindness tonight," Ian started as he seated me back at our table, "but I must be going now." He extended his hand forward, waiting for Nathan to clasp it in farewell. Nathan accepted his outstretched arm grudgingly, mumbling a farewell that was hardly intelligible. It was obvious Nathan was sulking.

Ian turned his attention back to me. "Callee, I hope your ankle heals quickly. And thank you for the dance." His face was lost in a shadow, and I could see nothing of his eyes now. There was no way to discern his emotion from his voice. I sat there in stunned silence.

I knew something on the dance floor had caused this sudden retreat, and my mind rebelled at the thought of Ian leaving right now. Before I could ask him to stay, Ian bowed and walked quickly towards the door. Moments later, he disappeared from sight, leaving me with nothing to do but wonder what I had gone wrong.

"Interesting fellow," Nathan commented. He was looking intently at my profile, trying to gauge my reaction to that comment.

I quickly veiled my real thoughts and turned to look at my best friend. "Yes," I agreed, "very interesting."

Before I could comment more, I was assaulted by the girls returning to our table.

"Oh my gosh, Callee," Amber gushed, sliding into a metal folding chair across the table. "He was gorgeous, li e a model straight from Hollywood. I mean, I didn't really get a close look at him from the dance floor, but wow! What did you talk about while you were dancing?"

"Did you see the way he looked at you Callee?" Kathryn picked up right where Amber had left off, taking the seat that Ian had vacated. "My heart nearly dropped when he touched your face. You looked like you were going to melt right there on the ground at his feet "What is he like?"

"Is he going to attend Cromwell?" Another voice, Rachel's this time, piped up. "I would love to sit next to him in Mr. Jenkins's class. It would certainly make the lectures more interesting."

Their eyes were sparkling, and I could feel a moment of jealousy well up inside me that I didn't quite understand. I felt like Ian was mine, for me and me alone. The idea that anyone else might also feel a special connection to him bothered me.

Jackie, at least, did not seem as enamored with Ian as the others. "Are you okay, Callee?" she asked real concern tinting her words. I gave her a grateful smile and assured her that I was fine.

I turned back to the other girls, determined not to be rude, and tried to answer as many questions as I possibly could, though they were coming at a fast and furious pace. Ian and I hadn't even talked for that long, maybe only forty minutes at best. I felt an odd sense of happiness that I could not share everything about Ian with them, since I only had limited knowledge of him myself. I wanted there to be something special just between the two of us. I did not want everybody to know Ian as I knew him.

I caught only a short look at Nathan's face as I talked, and it was evident that he was not happy about Ian's existence in West Liberty or the attention the newcomer was getting. I tried smiling at him, not only to lighten his suddenly sour mood but also to confirm our enduring friendship, but the glowering look never left his face. I was quickly pulled back into the conversation at hand, ending my quiet appeal to Nathan's good nature.

It wasn't long before the eleven o'clock hour hit, signaling the end of the dance. I was shocked how quickly the last half of the dance had passed. It seemed like the entire second part of the night had been engulfed by Ian's presence. Chaperons were ushering students out the front door, trying to get them home before parents started calling the school wondering where their children were.

Jackie took my arm, holding me behind the rest of our group as we walked back to the cars. When we were out of earshot, she leaned down and whispered in my ear, "Do you like him?"

I didn't even pretend not to hear her or feign innocence; I knew exactly who she was referring to.

I sighed. "I can't say that yet, but I certainly find him interesting." I was desperately searching for words to explain exactly what I was feeling.

Did I like him?

To be fair, I hardly knew the guy. I didn't know where he was from, anything about his parents, what hobbies he had if he played sports, or practically anything else. What did I really know'? He rescued clumsy women in distress, was an incredibly skilled dancer, couldn't hide his emotions, and was absolutely, irrevocably, drop-dead gorgeous. I laughed at my own ignorance. Still, the feelings I had, the emotions I felt, certainly went beyond platonic interest.

"I would really like to get to know him better," I finished lamely.

Jackie studied me for a moment, her blue eyes attempting to see-right through my forehead straight into my brain. She gave up her optical telepathy a few moments later and I saw a smile touch her lips.

"Still, he was good-looking, wasn't he," she said, giving me an all too knowing look.

I smiled back at my friend. "Incredibly," I admitted. To say the words out loud seemed to cement them in reality, and I was glad for the darkness that hid the red tinge covering my face.

We caught up with the rest of our group, already piled into the cars and were awaiting our presence to depart. Jackie and I were riding in separate vehicles, so I gave her a quick hug before turning to join my own troupe. I slid in the front seat, quickly rolling down my window to give the people sitting in the back of the car some fresh air, and thought again of Ian's warm hand touching my cheek. The evening breeze was cold as we wound through the streets of West Liberty, but the chill did nothing to cool the warm place where Ian's hand had rested.

~ 4 ~

I was flying. The landscape beneath me was still West Liberty, the people were the same, the scenery unchanged - and the boy in white linen was there again, watching. I promised myself that this time, no matter what, I would get a look at his face.

He flitted in and out of the sunlight, and I enjoyed the way the cloth hugged his body in the wind. I edged closer to him now. As if toying with me, he turned to float on his back, pointing his face upward to bask in the sunshine. I caught a glimpse of his facial profile, and felt myself draw in a sharp breath. It couldn't be! Certainly, my mind was playing tricks on me now, but there was no mistaking that squared jaw, straight nose, and dark blonde hair. Without glancing in my direction, he reached his hand towards mine, and I floated forward to grasp it. His head turned, his remarkable gray eyes meeting my own as a soft smile formed on his lips.

"Callee."

That voice again, smooth as silk, held me captivated. Only one word escaped my parted lips as I looked at the magnificent figure before me. "Ian."

Beep, beep, beep, beep, beep.

I sat suddenly upright in my bed, sitting there several minutes to allow my head to clear from its early morning confusion and willing myself back into reality. I realized my alarm was still beeping insistently and turned my body, stretching out my arm to smack the alarm clock, hard. Amazingly, my hand connected with the snooze button, stopping the offending noise at least momentarily.

Ian. I had been up half the night thinking about him, unable to fall asleep even after I crawled into bed. I had come up with a hundred unanswered questions while tossing and turning into the early morning hours. Apparently, sleeping had still done me no good as he had even managed to permeate my dreams. I swear I could still feel his hand in my own, the warmth of it transcending the barrier of the dream world. The dream had felt so real, and even now I could not quite shake the sensation.

Had he always been the presence in my dream since the beginning? Something inside me screamed yes, but how could I dream about somebody I had never even met before? It was more plausible that my subconscious had forced Ian there. After all, I had fallen asleep thinking about him. It was certainly reasonable for him to slide into my dream. "Yes," I finally decided, saying the words out loud to assure myself. That had to be the answer.

Feeling slightly more grounded, I turned and placed my feet on the floor. I gathered up my clothes for the morning and shuffled along the upstairs hall to the bathroom. Today was Sunday, which meant I had church this morning with my family. My early morning reverie had already put me behind schedule, and I could hear my parents and brother already chatting downstairs in the kitchen. Breakfast was frying on the stove, the smell wafting through the house causing my empty stomach to growl. I hurried through my morning routine, pulling my hair back into a messy bun before donning a brown, suede skirt and cream colored sweater. I slid into my favorite calf length brown boots before heading downstairs.

I hadn't more than walked in the kitchen before my mom bombarded me with questions about the Homecoming dance. Did I have a good time? Yes. Did I dance with Nathan? Yes. What did the decorations look like?

As I ate my eggs and toast, I recounted every detail for her. She smiled and nodded with a distant look, probably lost in some of her own memories. When I got up to the part about falling over my dress and Ian's remarkable rescue, my dad looked up from his morning newspaper. His light brown eyes gazed at me suspiciously. "What did you say this young man's name was?" he asked with a serious face.

I blushed, not liking the fact my father could read me so well. "Ian Evans," I answered looking down at my plate.

My dad thought on that for a moment, seeming to think something through in his head. Finally, he remarked, "I hadn't heard of any newcomers to West Liberty." With that, he went back to his morning paper. I let out a breath, thankful he didn't question me any further. It was that he hadn't heard of Ian before. My dad was the principal at Cromwell Elementary, and was usually the first to hear news from parents dropping their children off at school. I turned that over in my mind for a minute, then let it go, deciding it was not that important.

My mom also let the subject drop, but her look told me she would be hounding me again later in private.

The rest of my Sunday passed uneventfully. I sat in the middle of our pew at church trying to concentrate on Pastor Harvey's message. I had always liked the middle-aged man and found myself listening attentively to the sermon.

Our after-church routine was the same every week. We ate lunch and supper together as a family, and I usually worked on homework or did some reading in between meals. Today I changed into some comfortable jeans, then plucked a book off the shelf in the living room and settled myself in the shade of a maple tree in our backyard. I had read the same page several times, still not registering a word it said, before laying the novel aside and just enjoying the afternoon sunshine. No matter how hard I tried, those stormy may eyes were embedded in my head, and I knew it would be futile trying to do much today.

After supper that night, we watched a movie from our vast collection, breaking up afterwards so Jaden could start getting ready for bed. I told my parents I was going. To finish some homework and listen to music in my room before falling asleep. They both bid me goodnight as I headed upstairs behind Jaden. I fell into bed exhausted from lack of sleep two hours later, knowing Ian would be in my dreams waiting for me.

~ 5 ~

I waited impatiently outside Nathan's house Monday morning before school. We always walked together and I wasn't about to abandon him now, but I was eager to get to Cromwell today. Ian had said he was looking into starting classes here, and I wanted to know if he had made good on that. I wanted to see him in person.

That truth had hit me that morning as I was picking out something to wear. It had taken me an eternity to decide on the white, slim fit long sleeves and a faded pair of hip-hugging jeans. I had even taken extra time putting up my hair that morning, just in case. I had never been especially concerned about how I looked before, usually throwing on the first thing I saw in my closet and running out the door with a hairband in one hand and a piece of toast in the other.

I glared at Nathan's front door, mentally willing it to open. After what seemed like an eternity, I heard the creak of the hinges and Nathan appeared in the doorway, throwing me a smile and a wave as he loped down his walkway toward me.

"Good morning," he said cheerfully as he reached me. Nathan always woke up bright and chipper but crashed every night as soon as the sun went down.

"Good morning," I responded, as we turned and headed for the school. I was still a little worried Nathan might pick up where he left off the other night on the dance floor, but the conversation never moved in that direction. Instead, we talked about the latest English assignment, which was due in less than a week. English had always been one of Nathan's weak points academically, and he often tested out his report topic ideas on me, then had me proofread the paper for him once it was written.

We approached the school, blending in with the students now crowding the stairwell on their way to their lockers. I kept my eyes open, searching out the face I had thought about for the past two days and nights.

Nathan dropped me at my locker before continuing down the hall towards his own. I spun the combination and the door popped open. I bent down to retrieve my notes and the textbook I would need for first-period advanced algebra, all the while keeping my eyes on the hallway, looking for any sign of Ian. The sound of slamming locker doors signaled that class was about to start for the day. I sighed deeply, shutting my locker door before turning and trudging to class.

Jackie smiled and waved from down the hall, so I stalled to give her a return greeting before ducking into my classroom.

Through the entire period, I watched the door, hoping to catch a glimpse of blonde hair through the wire ridden glass pane. Still, there was nothing, and class ended without even a hint that Ian was here.

The four periods following played out almost the same way, with me watching the door only to be disappointed at the sound of the bell. I closed my locker door, preparing to make my way to lunch.

"Did you see the new guy," I heard as I passed by a small huddle of girls clustered around a locker. My pace immediately slowed as I walked by and my heart began its own marathon race in my chest.

"Yes," one other girl breathed, her face lighting up in obvious delight. "He looks like a model," she continued, the smile never leaving her lips, "and he has such remarkable silver eyes." I stopped moving completely.

The girls walked away then, their voices quickly becoming inaudible, but I didn't need to hear any more. They had already told me what I wanted to know. Ian was here.

I began walking again, letting my legs carry me forward through the hallway, down one flight of stairs, and onto the main floor. I stopped again just outside the cafeteria to steady myself. There were two periods set aside for lunch, with half the students eating in each timeslot, which meant there was a fifty-fifty chance Ian would be there right now.

Before I lost my courage, I stepped through the archway into the cafeteria. I scanned the crowd momentarily, and it didn't take me long to know that he was here, sitting on the far side of the room. It wasn't that I could see him, but it seemed half the students present had crowded around the table in order to talk with our newest arrival. Those that weren't immediately surrounding the table were looking in its direction, talking with their neighbor and pointing towards the gathering of students.

I hopped into the lunch line, maneuvering my body to catch a glimpse of Ian where he sat, but the assembly of students was too thick for me to see anything. Lunch today consisted of taco salad, corn, peaches, and milk, and I grabbed a tray even though I sure how much of it I would be able to eat. As I stepped out of the procession, I saw Jackie, Amber, Nathan, and a few of the other guys from our group sitting in the middle of the room. Jackie spotted me and waved, signaling me to come over and sit with them. I smiled, making my way in that direction.

I plunked my lunch down on the table beside Jackie's, making sure to sit so I could see in Ian's direction. I was five tables away from where he sat and craned my head trying to make him out through the crowd. Jackie followed my gaze and hid the smile that came to her lips, politely remaining mute on the topic.

"Hey Cal, how's it going? You haven't done anything disastrous today, like burning down the chemistry lab, have you?" This of course was from Nathan.

I looked at him and smiled sarcastically. "Not yet, but I don't have chemistry until seventh period," I joked. This drew chuckles from our entire group.

I didn't have to wait long for talk of Ian to surface. "Have you spoken to your knight in shining armor yet?" Amber had her eyes fixed pointedly at me as she asked the question, and I could feel all my friends' eyes shift in my direction.

"No, not yet," I admitted, trying to hide my discomfort at being the center of attention. "Actually, I only found out he was here while I was walking to lunch."

"I'm not surprised," Amber stated, "since he hasn't even sat through a class yet. I was working in the office helping answer phones while the secretary was on her lunch break when he came in to get his schedule. He looks even better up close than I had given him credit for."

"Did he say anything to you?" I asked, focusing on every word she said.

"Just good afternoon, he told me his name was Ian and that he was a new student, and he asked if he could get his class list. That was it."

I didn't know what I had expected, but the whole interaction sounded so ordinary. I guess I had been hoping for something that would give me more insight into Ian's personality. My stomach grumbled letting me know it was lunchtime, and I took a bite of my taco salad to appease the hunger gnawing at my insides. I chanced another look at the table, but Ian was still obscured from my view.

Nathan looked at me, frowning openly at the conversation. "I don't like him," he stated.

My eyes widened at his words. I had never heard Nathan say he disliked anybody before. Even if I was slightly enamored with Ian, Nathan certainly wouldn't hold that against the guy. Apparently, the rest of the table felt the same shock I did for nobody had moved a muscle since the outburst, each person just staring at Nathan in surprise.

Jackie was the first to voice what everybody else was thinking. "Why not?"

"He's hiding something." Nathan's words were direct, and despite my interest in Ian, I felt myself agreeing with Nathan's assessment. There was something the new student wasn't sharing. I had heard it in his voice at the dance and had seen it lurking behind his eyes.

The bell rang, breaking up the tense moment as we began gathering up our backpacks. While everyone was distracted I stole one last look towards where Ian was sitting. The crowd around him moments before had now dispersed, and Ian sat there, his silver eyes dead-set in my direction, watching me. I was held rooted to my seat by that gaze. He was dressed rather plainly, in denim jeans and a soft blue button-up shirt. Nevertheless, they looked superb on his well-proportioned frame.

I noticed the slight downward tilt of his lips as we looked at each other as if he was unhappy with something he saw. What could he be thinking? What could he be hiding?

Amber's insistent nudge broke through my trance, and I quickly picked up my tray and headed for the closest trashcan, glancing back one last time to find Ian's eyes still focused on me.

Tiny shivers of excitement ran up my back as I felt his gaze follow my retreating figure out of the cafeteria.

I had study hall next, so I swung by my locker to pick up some homework that needed to be done, then rushed to make it to the study hall room before the tardy bell.

I slid into my usual seat in the first row and opened my math textbook to the assignment due tomorrow. Somebody passed close by my desk on their way to their seat. I looked up just to see who it was and felt my heart slam into my ribcage. Ian breezed by me without a word or acknowledgment. He picked a seat two behind mine though he was one row over, and sat down, taking out a notebook and pen. He bent low over his desk and began writing furiously. His obvious brushoff made me angry.

Fine, if that was how he wanted it, two could play at that game. I returned my focus to the textbook on my desk and focused on the first problem. Though I told myself not to look, I couldn't help but sneak a peek at where Ian sat. He was still concentrating on the paper in front of him, but I saw him glance up every few seconds and look at me before putting his head down again and resuming his writing. In spite of my anger, I smiled at the knowledge that he was watching, then shifted my eyes back to my homework.

The bell rang, and I left the classroom before Ian had gotten up from his seat, feeling smug that I had returned his rejection. I made the customary stop at my locker to exchange books, then weaved my way through the crowded halls to chemistry.

I had barely crossed the threshold before spotting Ian sitting in the back of the science classroom next to the window. His eyes, which had been looking outside at the sunny afternoon, turned and looked at me now. The spot he occupied was once again two behind my assigned seat, and I hurried to plop down before I could be pulled in by his mesmerizing gaze. At least I knew one thing I hadn't before. Ian was definitely my age.

I could hardly concentrate on the lecture and was out of my seat the moment the bell sounded. After trading my books out, I made the dreaded walk to Mr. Jenkins's room, sitting down as quickly as I could. I stared at the door. Thirty seconds until class started. Fifteen. Each second seemed more like a minute to me. Ten. He wasn't coming. Five.

A dark blonde head appeared in the door, and I didn't know whether to feel relieved or angry as Ian's now-familiar figure shuffled to a seat two behind mine. Our routine of stolen glances continued through history. As the bell, at last, came marking the end of the day, I made up my mind — I would talk to Ian before leaving Cromwell. I rushed to my locker and threw my old books in while grabbing the ones I would need to do the rest of my assignments at home. I slammed the door shut and hurried down the hall, spotting him at a locker just a few feet ahead.

"Ian."' I said the name loudly, waving to get his attention. I saw him shut his door and turn to walk down the hall towards the front entrance. "Ian," I tried again, louder this time. His footsteps quickened, carrying him further away from me, down the steps, out the front door, and into the throng of students mingling outside, where I lost sight of him.

I stopped at the top of the stairwell, my heart crushed at what had just happened. He had heard me call out his name, of that I was sure. Obviously, he didn't want to talk to me or he would have stopped, and that rejection hurt me deeply. I went back into the hallway by my locker to wait for Nathan so we could go home together, a hundred questions spinning in my head. What did I do that made Ian hate me so'? What if even me at all, or was there something else pushing him away?

~ 6 ~

Sitting at lunch on Friday, I reviewed the past three days with a bit of disbelief. On my way to school Tuesday morning, I had made a promise to be mentally prepared for Ian's presence by the time lunch rolled around. With firm resolve, I had strolled into my first period class and almost cried in frustration when I saw Ian sitting two seats behind where I always sat. Second period was the same scenario all over again, and I soon discovered that Ian's schedule was identical to mine. We had class together every period and somehow Ian always managed to sit in the same spot behind me. I hadn't tried to talk to him after that first day, but I could always feel his eyes upon my back and often caught him looking at me before he had time to turn avert his eyes.

Even worse was watching the other girls in the school fawn all over him, hanging around his desk chatting away before class, sidling up to walk alongside him in the hallway, or crowded around him at lunchtime. I had burned with jealousy every time one of them batted their eyelashes in his direction, and what was worse was that he seemed not to mind their attention, chatting with every one of them quite easily and smiling the whole while. I was never close enough to hear what they talked about, but the idea that they were learning more about him than I would probably ever get to was driving me crazy.

I sighed as I dumped my tray and headed for study hall, ready to endure another class being ignored by Ian.

I slid into my seat and started pulling out my notebook and pen, waiting to catch a glimpse of Ian as he walked into the classroom. My pen hitting the desk matched the tempo of the seconds ticking by. The tardy bell sounded and I almost laughed thinking of Ian walking in late and getting a reprimand from the study hall monitor.

A minute went by, then two. I felt a frown now forming on my lips. Where was he? Three minutes. Four. After five minutes had passed without Ian appearing, I broke down and asked the monitor for a bathroom pass so I could look for him.

I slipped into the hallway, quickly making my way down the empty corridors and through the stairwells searching for Ian. I was on my second pass of the third floor and was nearing the end of the hall when I felt a cool breeze touch my face. I looked up and spotted the maintenance hatch that led up to the roof, noting that it was slightly ajar.

Everybody in the school knew the roof was off-limits to students and I had never before felt the need to defy that mandate. I stood at the bottom of the ladder which would allow me access to the roof, indecisive about what to do. I wanted to make sure Ian was okay but was it really worth getting in trouble for if I was caught?

I finally decided to throw convention to the wind, and after looking both ways to check for teachers, made my way up the ladder.

I pushed the hatch out of my path and hoisted myself up onto the rooftop. A chilly breeze whipped my hair around my face, and I had to use one hand to push it out of my eyes. It wasn't long before I spotted Ian's form outlined against the bright afternoon sun. He was standing on the ledge circling the roof, arms spread wide and eyes closed, his white shirt billowing behind him in the breeze. His face seemed to have softened as if he was completely at peace at the moment. The glow of his skin was mesmerizing and I stood still for a long time before making my way slowly towards him.

"So this is where you have been hiding," I said as I leaned on the ledge next to his feet, shading my eyes as I looked up at him.

He started for a minute at my voice, slowly lowering his arms back to his sides and turning his face downward to stare at me in silence. His gray eyes held me still and I caught my breath in anticipation. His body was poised to run at a moment's notice, and yet he did not move from his precarious balance on the ledge. His mind seemed to be battling with itself, one side demanding he leave me there alone and the other wanting him to remain.

"Not hiding," he said quietly as he turned his head back to face the sun. My heart leaped in my chest and I felt the air rush into my starving lungs. At last, Ian was talking to me.

"So what are you doing up here?" I asked, my mind commanding my heart to slow its rapid pace.

"Just taking in the weather," he said. The wind ruffled his hair and the sun highlighted the perfect features of his face.

I knew he was holding something back still. "And?" I probed.

He smirked. "I was giving us both a little space. Guess it didn't matter though since you followed me up here."

"I knew you were avoiding me the past few days," I started. "You left the Homecoming dance so quickly I thought for sure I had done something to upset you. Maybe you wouldn't mind enlightening me as to what I've done wrong," I finished breathlessly.

Ian turned to face me again and I was surprised at the pained look that crossed his face. His voice thickened, taking on a tone that sounded like sweet syrup dripping from his mouth. "If only

I could avoid you, Callee, but it seems we are being pushed to-gether. No matter how hard I try to stay away from you, try to keep from watching you, I can't seem to do it. I am sorry it is hurting you. It is hurting me as well." I believed him. His gray eyes were sad and I could read the emotion in them. "Don't worry Callee, you have done nothing wrong. Sadly, you are everything right, but you are dangerous to me in a way you can't possibly _ understand."

My heart leaped at those words. It was what I had wanted to hear all this time, yet Ian made it sound like a curse to have met me.

He was right about one thing; I absolutely did not understand his cryptic words. How could I be a danger to him? I did not want to hurt him. Could being with me really be hazardous?

"What is it?" I whispered, not trying to hide the confusion in my voice. "Why am I dangerous to you? You say I could not pos-sibly understand, but you haven't even tried to tell me what is going on? Maybe I could help you figure out a solution, and even if I couldn't, at least I would understand where you are coming from and why things have to be this way."

Ian groaned in frustration. "You do not understand what you are asking for. Life here is easy and simple for you. The things I know, the things I could tell you, would turn your world upside down."

Ian crouched down, his body shaking with each breath he took, and I saw him wrap his arms around his knees as if to hold himself together. "No, I cannot tell you Callee. It is better for us both that way. The closer you get to the truth, the harder it would be for you to understand when..." He left the sentence unfinished.

"When what?" I asked quietly. Despite everything he had al-ready said I wanted, no, needed desperately to know why we couldn't be together. Ian was downright afraid to tell me what he was thinking, but I knew no matter what secret he was keeping, nothing would stop me from being with him.

I waited anxiously to see if Ian would continue, but he didn't. Instead, he stood back up and began pacing along the eastern edge of the building. I watched his figure retreat to the corner, turn, and walk back. His gait was smooth and graceful like he was barely even touching the ground as he continued a second trip to the corner and back.

Whatever it was keeping us apart, it had to be big, beyond the scope of normal teenage problems.

From inside the school, I heard the sound of the bell signaling the end of class. Had it already been forty-five minutes? I panicked a little, knowing I would be reprimanded for skipping the entire study hall, but one look at Ian's face erased my fears. It had definitely been worth it for the chance to talk to him.

I felt my heart flutter in my chest as he made another round along the rooftop. He was beautiful, with eyes that held me captivated in their depth, and despite the secret, he held inside himself, I could tell his heart was pure. The mysterious air that shrouded him only added to his attraction, and I felt myself becoming lost in the moment as I gazed at his retreating figure. I had called him perfect once before and the word came rushing at me again without warning. I knew I would not survive going back to the way things had been between us, a place filled with only longing stares and marked silence.

That thought seemed to push me from the rooftop up onto the ledge where he was. There was no way I was going to let that happen.

Looking down at the ground below, I realized now how high up we were. I felt myself swoon a little and tried to take several deep breaths to keep myself grounded. When my head finally felt clear enough, I tried taking a step forward. The blowing wind made balancing a little difficult, but I adjusted my weight to accommodate its push. It was then Ian reached the corner and turned around to walk back towards me. I saw his eyes widen and his pace slow to a stop as he realized where I was standing. My eyes remained transfixed on his, and I took another step forward, then another.

"Callee, stop. What are you doing? It's dangerous for you to be up here." Ian's voice was worried, but I ignored his warning. My eyes remained transfixed on his, and I took several more steps forward. There were only a few feet of space left between us now.

Ian began walking then, closing the space between us. His step never faltered and the intensity in his expression sent a thrill through me. It was mere seconds before he was standing less than an arm's width away from me.

I didn't hesitate but reached out to take his hand in my own. The warmth I remembered was still there and spread from his body to my own as we stood there.

"Ian, you can tell me anything. It doesn't matter what it is, you don't have to protect me from the truth." I had never meant anything more in my life.

I saw him fight a desperate struggle with himself, the two sides of his conscious fighting with one another.

He groaned in apparent frustration, then bent his neck, touching his forehead to mine. The contact made my heart skip a beat and I could smell the faint mint of his breath as it brushed my face.

Ian closed his eyes. "It's not you I'm worried about most." I could hear the muttered words spoken between his ragged breaths. Without warning, he lowered his head, tilting his face to the side to capture my lips with his own. The kiss was slow

and sweet, surprising me only seconds before I felt my own response, closing my eyes and pressing in closer to deepen the
kiss. My free hand wound its way up around his neck, resting
there as the kiss went on. My hair was still caught in the breeze,
but I didn't notice. My mind was enraptured by Ian's kiss. The
warmth of his body seemed to have enveloped me, and I could
feel its warmth spread over me from head to toe.

Just as suddenly as it had happened, the kiss ended. I opened
my eyes and looked into Ian's, not quite sure what to say. His
eyes were stormy, pulled between what he felt and the reservations he had. I could see him desperately trying to regain control
of himself. Slowly, he untangled my arm from around his neck
and took a step back.

"I can't say I'm sorry Callee, but this can never be." Those
words tore at my body and my heart rebelled against them. I
knew he had enjoyed the kiss as much as I had and that he was
as intrigued with me as I was with him.

He let go of my hand then and averted his gaze.

My mind cried out, rebelling against his words, willing him to
trust me and tell me what was on his mind.

The sound of the hatch creaking open behind me caused me
to jump with a start. Somebody was coming. Ian and I were going to be caught on illegal territory. I started turning my body
around preparing to wait and be caught just as a strong gust of
wind came blowing from the west. My precarious balance on the
ledge was lost, and I saw Ian's face turn to shock as he reached
his hand out to catch me, but he was too late. I fell over the edge.

I was floating, but not the peaceful sensation that always ac-
companied my dreams. This time I was gripped with terror as I
saw the ground rushing up to meet my falling body. I heard myself scream, knowing it wouldn't do me any good but allowing it
to tear from my throat all the same. This is it, I thought desper-

ately. My life is going to end. I closed my eyes tight, waiting for the blackness to overcome my body.

I felt his hands gentle on my back and his chest hard beneath my shoulder as he cradled me close to his body. I must be hallucinating I thought wildly. But no, I could feel his warmth, same as always, spreading through my limbs. I opened my eyes. Ian's steely gray gaze stared down at me. We were still in midair, but the world falling up around me had slowed. What was happening?

I turned and saw the ground moving slowly closer. I looked back up at Ian's eyes, realization slamming into me like a train.

Ian was floating.

My mind tried to reject that thought, but as Ian's feet touched the ground as lightly as a feather falling to the floor, I knew it was true.

I looked at him with wonder in my eyes, a thousand questions forming in my head. Ian's own eyes looked down at me, pleading for understanding.

"What . . . how . . . ?" I couldn't seem to voice any of my thoughts. Normal people couldn't fly. It was obvious Ian was something else. Something not human.

"Are you okay? Do you think you can stand?" Ian asked quietly. I nodded, still not able to speak.

He turned my body, setting me gently upright on my toes and steadying me before releasing his hold. I stared at him and he stared back, neither of us moving or blinking for fear of startling the other person.

My voice caught up to me again. "Who are you?" I finally asked, my voice barely above a whisper.

Ian didn't speak at first, just looked at me as if to me gauge how much my startled mind could handle at the moment.

Finally, after a full minute had passed, he wet his lips and spoke three words which I will never forget.

"I'm an angel."

With that, he turned on his heel, striding away from me, away from Cromwell, and out of sight.

~ 7 ~

The next few days passed in a blur. I could think about nothing else except Ian's confession, the events of Friday replaying over and over again in my head. I knew it had happened and wasn't just a figment of my imagination. The very fact that I was sitting eating lunch with my family that Saturday afternoon was certainly a testament to that truth.

I shuddered inwardly. If Ian hadn't been there to save me, I would be dead right now.

Could what Ian have said even been true? Certainly, I had heard accounts of the existence of angels, but most of these centered-on guardians who were invisibly watching out for humankind, never about an angel pretending to be human walking in their presence for an extended length of time.

I saw Jaden give me a questioning look from across the dinner table, and I realized I hadn't said a word the entire meal. I smiled in his direction to assure him I was okay. That seemed to placate him, and he happily went back to his ham and cheese sandwich, recounting his latest adventure to our parents.

I was quickly lost in thought again.

Normal humans didn't fly, and being an angel certainly made more sense than man defying the laws of gravity. It would also explain why nobody had ever seemed to hear of Ian until the day he showed up in West Liberty. Still, it seemed impossible.

If he was an angel, it would explain the secret he had been hiding from everybody.

Stating you were an angel would probably be reason enough for public ridicule. I know I wouldn't have believed Ian if I hadn't seen substantial proof to make me think otherwise. And if you were an angel, would you really want anyone to know?

That thought brought on a whole other slew of questions. If Ian was what he claimed to be, why was he here in West Liberty? What was it about this place that demanded his presence?

"Callee?" I snapped out of my trancelike state at my dad's concerned voice. My family was looking at me expectantly.

"I'm sorry," I apologized with a smile. "I was thinking about something else. Could you say that again please?"

As soon as lunch was over, I disappeared to my room so I could continue my thoughts without the ever-watchful gaze of my family on me.

I had only been upstairs for a few minutes when I heard the house phone ring and my mom's voice speaking as she picked up the receiver.

"Callee, phone." Her voice echoed through the house, and I made my way downstairs to take the call. Could it be Ian?

I looked at my mom as she placed her hand over the receiver. "Nathan," she said softly, answering my unspoken question. I let my air out with a whoosh and took the phone from her outstretched hand.

"Hey Nathan," I said quickly.

"Hey yourself," he threw back. "What happened to you Friday? I waited for you after school, but you never came. Someone 'said you left sixth period and never came back. I thought maybe you got sick or something. Are you okay?"

I was touched by Nathan's concern. "I'm fine," I insisted. "I just left for the bathroom then ran into somebody I knew and lost track of time. I wasn't really itching to get back to study hall anyway."

At least I didn't have to lie about this, just omitted the finer details of the afternoon. No matter what, I was not going to tell Ian's secret, not that anyone would believe me even if I did.

Nathan laughed. "Callee, you've never ditched class before in your life. It's good to see you finally are human after all." He paused for a moment before asking why I hadn't met him after school.

In truth, I had been so shocked by what had occurred that I spent the rest of the afternoon in a daze I vaguely remember the study hall monitor yelling at me as I ran into the room to grab my backpack and I did not hear the lectures my teachers gave that afternoon or even notice the time until the final bell tolled. I left school immediately after the last period of the day and had forgotten all about Nathan.

"I just needed some solitude so I decided to walk home alone. I'm sorry, I should have told you what was going on," I apologized.

We chatted for a few more minutes before hanging up with the promise that we would see each other to walk to school on Monday morning.

I went back up to my room and put one of my favorite albums in the stereo system hoping it would distract me from thoughts of Ian.

It didn't work, and it wasn't long before I shut the music off again and began pacing back and forth across the soft carpet.

Even if everything Ian said was true, there was still one question burning in my head. He had said I was a danger to him. What had he meant by that?

And what had he meant by that kiss? I could almost feel his lips pressing against mine still, and felt myself shiver with delight.

The same questions repeated in my mind for the rest of the day, and by the time I crawled into bed, I was fairly dizzy from the thoughts circling around themselves in my head.

That night, I barely slept at all. When I did drift off for a few moments, all I saw was Ian.

Sunday arrived much too early, and I had to drag myself from the bed to the shower to get ready for church.

I went downstairs and poured myself a bowl of cereal for breakfast. My parents were busy hustling around the house getting ready still, and I was grateful for the silence in the kitchen.

The thoughts that had plagued me the day before continued to run in my head, and I knew today would probably be much like yesterday.

We sat in our customary spot at church. I tried to hide my yawns and hoped the pastor didn't see me and misinterpret the reasoning behind them.

It wasn't until we were walking out the door shaking hands with the greeters that I had an idea. I excused myself from my parents and walked down the hall to where Pastor Harvey was standing with a church family.

I approached the pastor, determined to get some answers to the questions plaguing me. I waited for him to finish his conversation and wave goodbye at the family before speaking.

"Pastor, I had a few questions for you. Do you have some time right now?" I threw the words out in a rush before I lost my nerve.

"Of course, Callee," he answered calmly, waiving me to his office down the hall.

I had only been in the pastors office twice before, but everything looked just like I remembered it. The desk took up a majority of the small room and had papers piled in neat stacks on top. There were two tall bookcases filled with books the pastor used as references for his sermons and a large potted fern occupied the corner of the room.

I sat in one of the two brown leather chairs which allowed me to look directly at the pastor from across the desk. There was a moment of silence as the pastor took his seat and folded his hands in front of him, leaning forward on his desk. He gave me a smile.

"So Callee, what can I do for you today?"

I swallowed heavily, feeling my determination quaver for an instant under the pastor's inquisitive eyes, but there was no turning back now. There were things I was desperate to know.

I pushed back my fear. "Actually pastor, I was really hoping you could tell me what the Bible says about angels."

There, I had said it. I put my hands in my lap, waiting to see what his response would be to my unusual request.

The pastor, however, did not seem taken aback at all. He smiled politely. "What exactly would you like to know?"

"I'm just looking for basic information. I know the Bible mentions angels, but maybe you could just stun up some of the information. You know, what's their purpose, what do they look like?" The words tumbled out of me, and I waited expectantly, excitement coursing through my body.

"Well Callee, there are many references to angels in the Christian text. While the Bible does not specifically mention the creation of angels, we know the earth was devoid of any existence before the creation account, so it is likely angels were created sometime within that seven-day time frame." He paused a minute, gathering his thoughts.

"There are several documented classifications of angels, including cherubim, seraphim, and the angels Michael and Gabriel. While these are the highest-ranked angels in heaven, the Bible does imply that there are multitudes of other angels there." He looked at me to make sure I understood what he was saying before continuing on.

"You asked what their purpose was. The word angel is actually derived from the word for messenger, and according to Scripture, an angel's sole purpose is to carry out the will, or message, of God."

I thought about this for a minute. If Ian was an angel and he was here in West Liberty, what was the reason for his presence? There were a hundred possible options and not all of them were good situations. I tried not to dwell on it for the moment and again looked at Pastor Harvey.

"Are there any accounts of angels appearing in human form?" This was probably the topmost question on my mind, for it was certainly a pivotal point to Ian's confession and the entire situation. I waited on the edge of my seat.

"Certainly so, but they also appear in many other forms as well. Angels have been documented taking on many shapes, and human forms are certainly among that list."

So, it was possible that what Ian claimed was the truth. That thought sent a wave of wonder through me, and I felt the reality of the situation crash down.

Ian was an angel, of that much I was now positive, and he was sent here to do something.

And he had kissed me. That thrill still hadn't escaped my thoughts and brought on even more questions than I had before. 'What about me was special enough for an angel to take notice, to care about me the way I knew Ian did? What possibilities were open to a human and an angel who liked one another?

Pastor Harvey's voice interrupted my thoughts. "The Bible also offers words of caution to those in the presence of angels."

"What do you mean?" I asked, fear gripping my insides. The grave look on his face let me know this was something serious.

"Not all angels are good, Callee. Remember, the devil was also an angel once but was thrown out of heaven, along with his followers, for thinking himself more important than God. See, many theologians interpret scripture as saying that angels have free will, like our own, which allows them to choose both paths towards and away from righteousness. When angels choose a path that contradicts the will of God, they are cast out of the midst of the righteous and down to earth." His eyes stayed on mine the entire time measuring my reaction to his words.

"Fallen angels are devious, Callee, and try to lead man into sin, away from the promise of heaven and into the darkness of hell."

His words sent a chill of alarm through me, but I thought of Ian's face and kindness and quickly suppressed my fear. I knew deep down that Ian was not one of the dark angels Pastor Harvey had mentioned.

"Is there anything else you want to know, or anything I can help you with?" His words were searching out the reason for this encounter, but I was not ready to let anyone else in on Ian's secret.

"No, but thank you for your time Pastor. It was really helpful." I stood up and shook his hand before leaving the room and returning to my parents and brother.

Our talk had made me feel a little better. At least I knew that I was not going crazy. I felt it now, the truth in Ian's words as if all the pieces of the puzzle were finally fitting together.

There were still some things I wanted to know, questions I knew only Ian could answer.

What was his purpose here? Was there any way I could help him?

Why was I dangerous to him? I could not accept his rejection of our connection without a reason.

Was there any way for us to be together?

I would find out the answers I promised myself as we drove home that day.

I suddenly felt better, lighter, than I had all weekend. Half the puzzle was solved, easing some of my anxiety over the situation.

The other half of the puzzle I would find out as soon as I could talk to Ian again.

A smile lit my face for the first time in days and I couldn't help the relief that now washed over my body.

Jaden seemed to notice my positive change in mood, quickly striking up a conversation about the
dinosaur he had found buried in our backyard.

As Nathan and I walked to school together Monday, I couldn't help but feel apprehensive. I knew Ian's secret now and there was certainly a chance he had left town after being found out. I prayed that wasn't the truth. I was ready to confront Ian to get the answers to the rest of my questions, but if he was gone, that was the end.

Nathan didn't talk and I was glad he seemed oblivious to my distraction that morning.

We neared the school and my eyes immediately began to search for Ian, scanning the faces quickly in the dense crowd. If he was here, he wasn't outside loitering with the other students.

I forced myself to calm down as I walked through the school's front doors. Just because he wasn't outside was no reason to get worried.

I still hadn't seen him by the time I reached my locker, and there were only a few minutes left until class started. My feet felt heavy as I wearily made my way to advanced algebra.

I was still fifteen feet away from the door when I sensed someone watching me from the other end of the hall. My head snapped up, but I knew before even looking that it was Ian.

Sure enough, he was coming from the other direction walking towards 01.11' first period class. His gait was graceful and he looked every bit as perfect as I remembered him. I felt myself grow excited as he looked at me. His face was somber and his eyes were searching my expression. I made my face as calm as I could, hoping he could see that what I knew had not scared me away. I tried to read the look in his eyes.

Worry? Fear? Nervousness? Excitement? The recesses of his gaze displayed all these emotions at once, and I was relieved that I didn't see anger there.

He reached the classroom before I did, giving me one last meaningful look before walking through the door. I stepped in the room and headed for my seat. As much as I wanted to talk to him, I knew this wasn't the place or time. There were too many people around who could overhear our conversation and I wanted us to be able to concentrate solely on each other when the right time came up.

That opportunity did not come quickly. By the time seventh period was nearing an end, I could hardly suppress the need to talk to him. I rushed to my locker, barely seeing the books I grabbed before practically running full speed to history class.

Ian was already sitting in his seat and I quickly took my place at my own grabbing a notebook and pen out of my bookbag. There was no way I would get to talk to Ian before school was out, and I was not going to wait any longer for the answers I needed or give him the opportunity to run away from me.

I began writing.

Ian, I need to talk to you, but not here. Where can I meet you after school?

I folded the note in half four times as the bell rang. I didn't know how I was going to get my message to Ian past Mr. Jenkins's watchful eye, but I would find a way.

I could hardly suppress my smile when I saw a substitute teacher come strolling through the classroom door. It seemed luck was on my side today.

The man wrote his name on the board and underneath wrote out chapters and pages we were to read in our history text before the end of class. The sub then sat down in his chair and lowered his eyes to several papers on his desk, not even looking at the students as people began opening their textbooks.

I took the opportunity to turn and toss the paper onto Ian's desk. He glanced at me quickly, then picked up the little note and unfolded it. I saw his eyes scan my writing. He looked at me again, and I stared back insistently.

Finally, he picked up his pencil and started writing something on the paper. I glanced at the teacher to make sure he still wasn't paying attention, then turned back towards Ian.

He had refolded the note and was now reaching in my direction, the slip of paper in his outstretched hand. I took it from him and opened it.

His neat handwriting was dark against the white background.

I don't know if that's a good idea. Maybe it is best for us to stay away from each other:

I didn't hesitate, but scrawled a quick message to him and tossed the note back to his desk.

No way. There is one reason we met. I am not afraid. Just tell me when on where?

Even we meet, if you learn the answers to all your questions, it will still not change the way things have to be. The closer we are to each other, the harder it will be in the end. Are you sure you can handle that?

Who says things have to be this way? There are always options Ian. At least try. Even if nothing changes, it is worth the risk to me. There is something special between us, and I don't want to lose that. Now, where are we going to meet?

Do you know how to get to the swinging bridge over Coldwater Creek?

I turned my head and nodded to him, slipping the note into my binder.

The swinging bridge was back in the woods surrounding the city park, about a fifteen minute walk from Cromwell.

"After school," I whispered quietly before turning back to the front of the classroom.

I felt excitement course through my body. At last, Ian and I were going to be alone.

I suddenly could not wait to get out from under the fluorescent lights of the school and I glanced at the clock anxiously. Only thirty minutes left until the end of class.

The time would go faster if I was busy. I decided to work on the reading assignment, but couldn't seem to focus fully on the pages in front of me.

Twenty minutes left.

My muscles tensed in frustration. Surely it had been more than ten minutes.

I tried reading the text again, willing my head to focus on the words in front of me. It seemed to work, and when I looked at the clock again there were only five minutes left. Four. Three. I packed up my book bag, knowing I wouldn't get anything more done today. The bell rang and I looked at Ian before slinging my backpack over my shoulder and heading out the door.

At last, I would get my answers.

~ 9 ~

I didn't see Ian on my walk to the woods and it made me nervous. What if he decided not to come?

He certainly had no reason to trust me with a secret he was obviously trying to hide, especially since we had only met him a little over a week ago.

I shook my head to clear my thoughts. I couldn't worry about that now though; I had asked him to meet me and he had agreed. Now the only thing left to do was go forward and hope he hadn't changed his mind.

I made it to the edge of the woods and located the trail that would lead back to the swinging bridge. The foliage around me was dense as I plunged into the dark green undergrowth and made my way down the narrow dirt path.

I had never been particularly fond of the woods. There were too many horror stories involving people who got lost in the forest and were never found again. I couldn't help the dread that overtook me and didn't stop myself from looking both ways, scanning the woods for any signs of attack.

My fear was unwarranted and I didn't see anybody hiding behind a tree waiting to ambush me. I kept my guard up anyway, prepared just in case.

It wasn't long before I heard the trickle of water up ahead, and I quickened my pace in anticipation. The trees thinned out around me and I saw the ropes attached to cement pylons which marked the beginning of the swinging bridge.

The structure was fairly old, dating back almost a hundred years, but you couldn't really tell by looking at it. The city maintained the bridge, replacing old wood planks and the ropes as needed to keep the structure in good condition. It was higher on the ends but dipped low, closer to the creek, in the middle. The system of ropes was intricate and supported the wooden planks below while creating hand rails at arm height, with ropes crisscrossed between the two extremities to keep people from slipping through the side.

I stepped up to the wooden planks, and let out a slow breath. Ian was already here, sitting in the middle of the bridge, his feet dangling over the edge and his arms looped around the ropes at his sides. The slight glow that was always around him seemed brighter in the shade of the trees.

The bridge swayed and creaked as I walked out onto the structure, and Ian turned, his eyes penetrating my approaching figure. I walked slowly, trying to keep my balance as the bridge rocked to and fro, and finally reached Ian in the middle. I took a deep breath then sat down beside him, letting my feet drop over the edge to dangle alongside
his. I looked straight ahead, not letting myself be distracted by his presence.

"I'm glad you came," I started out, not quite sure what to ask first.

"I shouldn't have," he replied, his eyes never leaving me.

I couldn't help it. I looked at him then.

We were sitting very close and I couldn't help but think of the other times we had been this way. The memory of the kiss burned inside me.

I wouldn't start with that question I decided.

Before I had even decided what to ask, Ian spoke. "Thank you for not telling anybody about me. I wasn't sure what to expect when I came to school today, but nobody mentioned anything to me about angels or flying. You have no idea how much that means to me." His smooth voice flowed over the words and his eyes displaying his gratitude.

I stared at him feeling slightly astonished. "Of course, I wouldn't tell anybody. For one thing, they wouldn't believe me even if I did. I would just come off sounding crazy. And secondly, it is not my secret to tell. Whatever your reason is for being here, I know it is not to harm anybody. Why should they need to know something like this if it is not going to harm them?" I finished my tirade slight out of breath. I wasn't sure what he thought of me, but I certainly wanted him to know I could be trusted.

"You are amazing," he said, his eyes taking in my face as if I was the most incredible sight he had ever seen. I blushed at his words.

"Of the two of us, I don't think I'm the amazing one," I replied.

We stared at each other for a second before Ian started talking again.

"I know you came here to get some answers, Callee." He looked away from me as if to hide from what was coming.

I tried to think of how to start without asking something too deep first.

"Maybe you could just tell me about yourself. I must -admit my knowledge of angels is limited, so make it as basic as possible," I offered.

He looked a little relieved as if he had expected that question.

"I have existed almost since the beginning of time. You cannot even imagine what it is like to see the Earth created before your very eyes, to see oceans separate from land, to watch day turn to night, and for stars to appear in the sky from nowhere. To see man-made from the dirt of the earth, to watch humans multiply in number, to see how things change over thousands of years. It is inspiring and incredible to behold."

Ian was lost in the moment that was his alone. He was right, I could not even fathom what that was like. I had certainly seen things change, but they were trivial matters in the scope of what Ian was talking about now. I could not even imagine the wonder of it all.

"Have you ever heard that angels have a rank in heaven?" he asked me.

I nodded, thankful I had talked to Pastor Harvey. At least I could keep up with some of the things Ian was saying.

"I am one in the multitude of unranked angels. I don't have a specific purpose or function, but perform a variety of tasks as commanded."

My next question seemed to follow naturally with the progression of the conversation. "So what are you doing here in West Liberty?"

Again, Ian looked like he had expected this question.

"I was sent here to watch over the town, or more specifically, the people living here. I wasn't given explicit instructions when I was sent, just to watch over everything and interject if somebody was in trouble. That was part of the reason I started attending Cromwell. It is much easier to keep an eye on people if you are where they are."

I nodded at his summarization. It only made sense to follow those you were looking out for.

"You might think this is a strange question, but I am curious . . . aren't angels supposed to have wings?"

I had been ready for him to laugh, but his serious face surprised me. "We all have wings."

He stalled for a minute and I could see he was trying to find the best way to explain things to me.

"They are hidden, what you might call invisible. You see, an angel's wings are a source of power. The only time they become visible is when that power needs to be displayed. Like the wings, an angel's power is hidden, lying dormant until needed."

"What is this power?"

"It differs. The power is individual."

"And what is your power?"

He went quiet immediately, and I regretted asking something that was obviously a sore subject.

"I'm sorry," I finally managed. "You don't have to answer that if you don't want to."

"No, it's okay," he said, choking on the words. "It's just that I don't know what my power is. I have never seen my wings before. Some angels go without ever discovering their true power; they just never need to use it."

His silence was telling, and I tried desperately to think of another question that would distract him from what he must have considered a failure.

"Is Ian Evans your real name?"

I had been thinking about this question almost since I had found out the truth about him. The way he looked at the Homecoming dance before giving his name had piqued my interest even then, and when I thought about it compared to the reality of the situation, my curiosity had grown.

I was surprised at the flush that spread across Ian's face.

"Actually," he began timidly, "I really don't have a name where I am from. I had to make one up if I was going to be here for a while and be able to blend in."

I nodded again. It was a logical assessment and I was glad to have a name to associate with this incredible boy beside me. Ian seemed to suit him.

"If you are alone here, where are you sleeping?"

"This is my home," he said smiling as he gazed at the woods surrounding us. "I sleep here around the bridge every night. It is wonderful, always being enclosed by the beauty nature reveals to us. I don't think people ever take enough time to be thankful for the world around them. This place was created to be admired, yet humanity treats it like a tool to be used and discarded at their disposal. It's sad." I could tell he meant what he said. His face was somber as he revealed his thoughts to me.

"What is it like to be human? Is it what you expected?" I couldn't help but wonder about this as the weekend went by. It certainly must be different for him.

Ian looked directly into my face, his gray eyes looking deeply into my own.

"As angels, we often hear about human emotions, how they are strong beyond the point of distraction. It seems like such an abstract idea to us," he answered quietly.

"Being here, now, I can't help but be assailed by the emotions one person can hold. They are intense and hard to control, like a cup of water running over. Feelings of anger, joy, sadness, jealousy, want..."

He trailed off, but I caught the unmistakable look in his eyes and my heart was pounding. I knew he was talking about the way he felt for me, the feelings he had when we were together.

"Don't look at me like that," he commanded quietly, but I could hardly control the feelings flooding me.

"Why am I dangerous to you?" The pleading question came out barely above a whisper.

I was desperate. Desperate to know why he was fighting so hard to stay away from me, why it was so important for us to be apart.

He didn't answer right away, but slowly reached out and took my hand in his, holding it tightly, letting the warmth of his palm flood through me.

"Callee." His voice was broken and his expression was softer than I had ever seen it. I could see he was troubled by my reaction to his words. His gay eyes were practically molten in their intensity.

"When I am with you like this, when we touch, when you look at me, I can't concentrate on anything else. Not the people I am here to protect, not the mission I was sent on, not even where "I came from."

I could sense there was more and I waited patiently for him to continue.

"I will not be here forever." The words were dragged from his mouth and I could tell he wished it weren't so.

"One day I will be called away from West Liberty, away from this world and back to a realm where you cannot possibly follow me."

I could sense myself panic at what he was saying. I barely remembered what my life was like a week ago before Ian came into it. Everything had changed so quickly. A world without Ian . . . I didn't even want to imagine it.

"I cannot ignore the call when that time comes. Angels who rebel against their command are thrown from heaven, left to wander the earth aimlessly as one of the fallen, or worse, join the side of darkness."

I shuddered, remembering the foreboding I had felt as Pastor Harvey had mentioned the fallen angels yesterday in his office.

"When I am here with you Callee, I want nothing more than to remain by your side, but the cost of that decision is too great for me to make."

I didn't take my eyes of his as he finished. "In the end, I will leave this place, and the closer we are to each other, the harder it will be for me to leave, and the more you will be hurt in the end. I do not want to see you in that kind of pain. Can you understand that?"

He was pleading with me now, his gay eyes tortured as he begged for me to realize his position and my own.

My head was swimming with all the information he had given me and I had to quiet my mind in order to focus on what he asked.

As much as I wanted to hate him for not promising to stay with me, I could not bring myself to fully feel that sentiment. This was hurting him as much as it was me.

He untangled his hand from mine and rested it lightly on my cheek, forcing me to meet his gaze. Ian had turned his body so that he was now fully facing in my direction.

"Please tell me you understand," he said again.

"I understand." I could do nothing else to assure him as my heart felt like it was being torn in two, but I hoped hearing the words would be enough to ease his distress. I wasn't mad, but I couldn't keep the sadness from registering in my eyes as a lone tear fell down my cheek.

Ian's face was torn as he wiped away the moisture.

"If things were different, there is nothing that would stop me from staying with you. I hope you know that." His last words were meant to be comforting, but they only made the pain raging inside my body worse.

The sound of distant thunder made Ian's gaze turn westward. I also looked, and the dark clouds heading our way promised a storm before the end of the evening.

Without a word, Ian stood and offered me his hand.

"We better get you home before it rains. I don't want your parents to be worried." He spoke the words as he pulled me to my feet.

I stretched my muscles which had cramped up from sitting too long in one spot. We began to head back through the woods towards the city park.

Ian did not release my hand, though neither of us spoke as we walked.

It wasn't long before we were walking down Main Street and turning onto Westbrook Drive.

We stopped in front of my house, but I did not let go of Ian's hand, and he didn't try to walk away. I didn't want this moment to end, but I wasn't sure what to say to make the time last longer.

"Ian." My voice was thick, the unshed tears seeming caught in the back of my throat. "I know we can't be together, but I would still like for us to be friends while you're here."

I thought Ian would say it wasn't a good idea, that it would be too hard to resist our connection we spent more time together. I held my breath waiting for -the rejection.

"Alright."

I looked up into Ian's face surprised. His smile was drawn, but he had agreed.

He must have seen the question in my eyes.

"Even if I try to avoid you Callee, it will do no good. We are always being thrown together even when we try to avoid each other. Maybe we will quit having such eventful run-ins if I don't try and stay away from you."

I laughed a little in spite of myself. At least I would be able to talk to him in person during school. I bid him goodnight as I turned and walked to my house. I slipped through the front door and ran up to my room before my parents could detain me.

I ran to the window in my bedroom that faced the street and parted my curtains to look out in front of my house.

Ian was still standing there, staring at our front door with a longing look on his face. He didn't move for several more minutes, just staring at the place where I had disappeared into the house.

Slowly he turned and walked back toward Main Street with his hands in his pockets and his head down staring at the sidewalk. I watched him until he was out of sight, then turned and threw myself on the bed to cry all the tears I had locked inside until now.

~ 10 ~

While I was worried my tentative truce with Ian would not hold, he was good to his word and I found myself talking with him almost every day over the next two weeks, though we were never alone again after that time at the swinging bridge.

The more I learned about Ian, the harder it became not to get attached to him. I could still read every emotion he felt when I looked into his silvery eyes, and I would often find myself staring at him just to grasp what he was thinking. Those eyes could dance with happiness, burn with anger, and soften with understanding all in an hours' time, and I drank in each moment, storing it away in the back of my mind. I daydreamed about him almost constantly and was reprimanded by more than one teacher for my lack of focus.

I would sometimes catch him staring at me with a yearning look in his eyes, but as soon as he saw me watching, he would quickly mask the expression with a cheerful smile and busy himself with some other task.

I knew by being together as friends and growing closer to each other every day, we were only making it harder to deny the attraction between us, but I couldn't help myself; I wanted to be near him. It was getting harder to deny the way I felt for Ian, and I knew that being near him if only as a friend, was better than not being near him at all.

My other friends were not oblivious to the change between Ian and me and would ask me every day if there something was going on between us. Though I would unwaveringly deny anything beyond friendship, it was obvious they didn't believe me.

I had finally invited Jackie to my house one day and admitted that I liked Ian so much it hurt, pouring out almost every detail of our conversations together. I conveniently left out the part about Ian being an angel.

She had listened intently, asking questions in all the right places and offering sympathy where needed, but in the end, she was able to offer no better solution to my dilemma. Still, it was nice to talk to somebody else about my feelings for Ian.

Of all my friends, Nathan seemed especially interested and he cornered me one day on our way home from school, demanding to know exactly what was going on between Ian and me.

"Nothing Nathan. We are just friends." I gave the well-rehearsed answer without blinking, but couldn't help the frustration from showing on my face. Nathan read my expression, not fooled by my response. After that, he kept a watchful eye on both Ian and me.

Despite my unbridled emotions, the days passed without fanfare, slipping by as if nothing unusual was happening.

It was almost hard to believe Ian was an angel. He acted so normal every day at school, never giving away what he really was to any of our fellow classmates. To anybody else, Ian appeared exactly as he wanted, an ordinary seventeen-year-old high school student.

I knew the truth though, and stories were rolling in every day proving that he was busy in West Liberty.

One day, before history class started, I overheard Katie Henderson talking with her friends about a fire that had broken out in the pizzeria uptown, which her dad owned.

"It's strange," she said, her brow furrowing in concentration, "but my dad swears he saw somebody holding a fire extinguisher putting out the flames in the kitchen. He was too busy trying to get everybody out of the restaurant to stop and thank the person, but when he went back to say it later, the person was gone."

I had looked over to where Ian sat nonchalantly at his desk, knowing full well that he was the mysterious firefighter from the pizzeria.

Ian was looking back at me, his gray eyes silently ' pleading with me not to say anything.

Another one of my classmates, Kendra Stutzman, had been walking to the supermarket to pick up some groceries for her mom. As she was crossing Main Street, a car came speeding down the road, blowing the red light and heading straight at Kendra.

Kendra was standing in the lunch line telling the story to a wide-eyed Nathan. "I was so surprised I didn't move. There is no way the car missed me. Somebody ran up to me and I felt hands on my arm, pushing me out of the road. I fell, I was only down for less than a minute, but when I stood up and looked around, nobody was there. The doctors thought I hit my head and imagined it, but I know I felt somebody's hands push me."

It seemed that every time a dangerous situation was dispelled, the mysterious rescuer went missing before anyone ever saw him or her.

Some of the students had laughed at all the stories, swearing there was a ghost in West Liberty that went around saving people.

They were wrong.

Other students swore a guardian angel must be watching out for them.

They were closer.

September passed into October almost uneventfully, and talk of the mysterious guardian angel dimmed as students began eagerly discussing fall break, which was only one week away.

Every year during fall break the school hosted a three-day trip to Sandy Point State Park in Annapolis, Maryland for all junior and senior students. One of the highlights of being an upperclassman was getting to go on the fall break trip. Many students considered it the final farewell to warm weather before fall truly set in.

The buses left on Thursday evening after school and came back Sunday night. The bus ride only took five and a half hours, and students always arrived at the park in time to set up their campsites before sunset.

The park was packed with activities, including swimming, fishing, hiking, canoeing, and kayaking, and students were given free rein to do whatever they wanted within the park boundaries.

There were a few requirements on the trip. One was to let the chaperones know what activities you and your group of friends planned to do on that day and where you would be doing them. Occasionally people got lost inside the park, and it was easier for the rangers to find you if they had a basic idea where you might be. Also, students were required to check in with chaperones at every meal and before twilight, and after dark, all students were required to be at their designated campsite (co-ed tents not permitted). Besides these three rules, the standard code of acceptable conduct applied, and if for any reason you were caught causing trouble, you were immediately sent to the leader's tent and would remain there for the rest of the trip. This almost guaranteed that students behaved themselves while at the park.

This would be my first year going to Sandy Point, and I couldn't hold back my excitement as I talked with Nathan and Jackie about what we should do while we were there.

I wasn't sure if Ian planned on going to Sandy Point, but I wasn't going to let his presence deter my enjoyment of the weekend. Still, I couldn't help but ask him the Tuesday before the trip what his plans were for fall break.

"I heard about the class outing to Sandy Point," he began, looking at the slice of pizza on his lunch tray while he talked.

Lately, he had gotten into the habit of avoiding my gaze by looking down while he spoke, but I tried not to let it bother me. If it made things easier for him I would bear it, but I missed the soft, silvery look of his eyes.

"And?" I prompted quietly.

"I think I am going to go," he finally said, chancing a quick look in my direction before dropping his eyes again.

I couldn't help the happiness that bubbled up inside me. "That's wonderful Ian. It's supposed to be beautiful there. I'm sure you will love it." I thought of Ian's appreciation for the outdoors, the way he had looked that day on the roof with his arms spread wide, and couldn't help the smile that broke out on my lips. He would definitely enjoy the state park.

"Thanks, Callee," he said, his eyes looking at me in earnest now. "I thought I might ruin your time there if I went, but I want to be able to keep an eye on the students on the trip."

I gave him a light punch on the arm. "Don't be silly Ian. We are friends. I am glad you are going to be there."

The thought of a weekend away from West Liberty was exciting, but having Ian with me made the idea even more appealing. The bell rang signaling the end of lunch and Ian and I rose together, dutifully returning our trays to the kitchen before heading to study hall together.

~ 11 ~

One week later, I couldn't contain my excitement as the last bell rang. I practically flew out of my seat into the crowded hallway, laughing as I saw many of my classmates doing the same thing. All the upperclassmen were as excited as I was to leave West Liberty behind for the weekend.

I threw my whole backpack into my locker and grabbed my overnight duffel bag, slamming the metal door closed with a bang. I made my way out to where the buses were parked, ready to transport the student to Sandy Point for the weekend.

I spotted Jackie in the crowd of students and waved as I jogged in her direction. We had agreed to sit together on the bus for the five-hour trip. Amber and Kathryn were going to try and get the seat behind us, and Nathan and the guys were going to try and take up the seats across the aisle. I wonder where Ian will sit, I mused silently, looking for his unmistakable presence among the throng of students.

The buses were typically divided up by class, with the seniors taking up the front bus and the juniors riding in the second. Jackie and I made our way to the back bus, handing off our bags to the chaperones, which consisted mostly of teachers from Cromwell, to stash away in the storage space beneath the bus.

All the seats in the back of the bus had filled up already, which wasn't unusual since the teachers usually rode in the front, so Jackie and I made our way to the middle, being sure to leave room behind us and beside us for our friends.

The air was hot and stifling in the enclosed space, and Jackie opened the small window beside her to allow the fresh breeze in.

Students continued to board the bus, laughing and jostling one another good-naturedly as they made their way down the center aisle. Our friends were soon sitting, taking up most of the seats surrounding us, and we began an animated discussion of what to do at Sandy Point first.

I knew the moment Ian entered the bus. The boisterous talking became more hushed as girls started whispering to one another.

"I didn't know he was coming."

"Look at those eyes."

"I hope he sits back here."

"You know he's not seeing anybody yet."

"I wonder if he likes somebody at Cromwell."

I caught pieces of the conversations swirling around me, and looked up, my heart caught in my chest.

Like the girls around me, I couldn't help but admire Ian's remarkable gay eyes, flawless features, and amazingly toned body. Ian's eyes flashed in my direction, and he smiled politely when he caught my stare.

I blushed but managed a smile and a wave in spite of my embarrassment at being caught staring.

I held my breath as Ian made his way towards me, his eyes never leaving mine, finally stopping at the seat across the aisle and one in front of mine and smoothly sliding into the empty space beside an astonished Nathan.

I giggled under my breath, imagining the death looks Ian was sure to get on the trip to Maryland.

It wasn't long after that the teachers boarded the bus and began taking down the names of all students present, checking them against the roster attached to a clipboard in their hands.

Many parents had shown up to send off their children, and I caught sight of my family on the sidewalk, waving as they spotted me through the glass window. Jaden was jumping up and down, brandishing his arms wildly, and I laughed and stuck my hand out the window to return their farewell.

I turned back to the front, shocked to see Ian looking at me intently, a warm smile on his face. I blushed furiously as I reached into the small bag that held my mp3 player, glad for something to do too busy my hands.

I put the headphones over my ears and scanned until I found my favorite songs, letting it play softly in my ears.

A cheer went up around me and I looked to see the sign proclaiming Welcome to West Liberty pass by on the right-hand side of the bus.

The gentle sway of the vehicle and the soft music soon lulled me to sleep, only to wake two hours later as the bus hit a large bump in the road, throwing me against Jackie's body, making us both laugh.

I looked up to see if Ian and Nathan were talking, surprised to see them both asleep despite the jostle that had woken me moments before. Nathan was slouched in his seat, leaning up against the window with his arms crossed loosely across his chest. He often fell asleep on the bus during long field trips, and his posture hadn't changed since we were in grade school.

I looked at Ian, taking in a sharp breath as I did so. He was sitting almost upright, his head leaned back against the green plastic of the seat and his face turned in my direction. The late afternoon sun caught his dropped eyelashes, casting long shadows across his cheeks. I saw the steady rise and fall of his chest, noticing his broad shoulders lift and drop smoothly with the repeated action. His features were soft in sleep, his mouth slightly parted by the relaxed pose, drawing my attention to his smooth lips.

My cheeks flamed, remembering all too well just how smooth and insistent those lips could be.

The music was still playing in my earphones, and I rested my head on the seat behind me once again, drifting into another uneasy nap.

It had been weeks since I had my last dream, but I recognized the familiar sensation immediately.

Ian was beside me, gliding effortlessly in and out of the clouds, smiling contentedly.

I tore my eyes away from him, looking at the town of West Liberty below me. Something wasn't right. The town was still there, but there was something different from my previous dreams. It took me a while to realize that there were no people, no cars, no signs of life on the streets.

I looked back up at Ian, noticing for the first time the dark black clouds rolling in behind him.

"Ian," I shouted in warning, my voice coming out slightly muddled in the dream.

He didn't hear me. "Ian," I yelled again, louder this time, trying to catch his attention.

Things seemed to happen in slow motion. Ian turned to look at me, his face registering surprise at my tone of voice. I pointed at the sky around us, his gaze following my motion to the dark clouds now closing over West Liberty.

He turned to me again, flashing me a smile of understanding.

Suddenly, a bolt of lightning flashed from the sky. I stared in awe at the streak of light, bright violet, unlike any color I had ever seen before.

Ian's face blanched white with shock as the lightning pierced his right shoulder. I saw him clutch his arm and cry out in pain, then slowly begin to fall, dropping out from my line of sight before I had time to react.

"Ian! Ian, NO."

"Callee. Callee, wake up."

Someone was shaking me hard, their soothing voice veiled with concern.

My eyes flew open, taking in the worried faces of my friends crowded around me. Ian's hands were still on my arms, worry etched in every part of his face as he looked at me searchingly with his gray eyes.

"Callee, are you okay?" Jackie's fearful voice asked, and I turned to look at her. My heart was still beating ferociously and my breath was coming out in heavy pants. I took a deep breath to steady my calm nerves and turned back to face Ian, reassuring myself that he was okay.

"I'm okay," I said, finally feeling calm. Though I spoke the words to everyone, I was looking only at Ian.

"What happened Callee?" Nathan asked quickly. "You were tossing and turning in your seat. You were practically shouting by the time Ian decided to wake you up.

"It was just a bad dream," I said, recalling the terror I had felt only moments before. A shudder went through my body and Ian tightened his hands protectively around my arms.

"What was I saying?" I asked, afraid of the answer.

All eyes went to Ian and he smiled ruefully at me. I dropped my head to my hands, hiding my blush behind openly splayed fingers. I had definitely called aloud to Ian.

"I'm okay," I said again, lifting my head and letting a watery smile form on my lips.

My friends dutifully sat back in their seats as a chaperone began making her way down the aisle towards us to see what all the commotion was about.

Ian still didn't let go of me, his eyes looking pointedly at me, holding my gaze steadily.

"Are you sure you're okay?" he asked one more time, glancing behind him at the teacher closing in on us.

I leaned down, touching my lips almost to his ear, making sure that nobody else was listening.

The scent coming off Ian's skin was mesmerizing, and I inhaled deeply before quietly whispering, "Ian, I need to talk to you, alone."

He nodded at me. "Wait for me after lights out."

Ian quickly slipped back into his own seat just as the teacher arrived to investigate.

~ 12 ~

The last two hours to Sandy Point passed in a blur. Before I knew it, we were pulling into the park entrance, registering our group's arrival with the lady stationed in the home office before making our way to the campground.

The students began piling out of the buses, glad to stretch their cramped muscles after the long journey. Jackie and I picked up our luggage and the tent that was ours for the weekend, waiting patiently for Amber, Rachel, and Kathryn to catch up with us before heading to the girl's half of the campsite. There were minimal daylight hours left, so we wasted no time setting the tent up and unrolling our sleeping bags inside before heading to the picnic area for supper.

Nobody was allowed to leave camp on the first night, so many students stayed around the picnic area after dinner playing cards or other games until they were sent to their tents for the night.

I watched my group of friends play several rounds of euchre in the waning evening sun, waiting anxiously for the chaperones to call lights out. Ian was in a clearing just outside the picnic tent watching a pick-up football game the boys had organized, and I kept shooting looks in his direction, willing the time to go faster.

Thankfully, I didn't have to wait long. Half an hour later, we were shooed back to our campsites. Ian caught my eyes and gave me an imperceptible nod before disappearing into the darkness.

We all trudged wearily back to our campsite, bidding the boys goodnight before crawling into the tent and dropping onto our open sleeping bags. I listened quietly, waiting for the telltale breathing that let me know the other girls had fallen asleep. It was almost an hour before I quietly slipped from my sleeping bag and out into the starlit night.

Insects were chirping noisily in the trees surrounding me, and I sat silently outside my tent, listening to their wondering how long it would be before Ian would join me.

The dark night around me only reminded me of the rolling, black clouds from my dream, and I shuddered involuntarily.

The hand that snaked out around me, closing quickly, but softly, over my mouth surprised me. I almost screamed, but quickly stifled it as I felt the warmth of Ian's hand and recognized his distinguishable scent.

He felt my body relax and released me. I turned to see him crouched on the rights side of the tent entrance, his body hidden in the shadow created by the moon. He beckoned with his hand for me to come join him in the dark, and I followed without hesitation.

I sat beside him in the shadow, acutely aware of our close proximity. Ian also seemed affected by our nearness, and I could sense the emotions warring within him.

In the dark he seemed even more unearthly, his gray eyes luminous, shining even without the sun, and his skin still giving off a slightly radiant glow.

I took a deep breath then launched into the details of my dream on the bus, telling him everything I could remember. Ian listened intently as I recounted the story for him, not moving an inch until I had finished the tale.

"That's not all Ian," I said, looking at my hands wringing in my lap. I then told him about my first set of dreams, about flying over West Liberty and sensing his presence beside me. I could feel my cheeks flaming in the darkness.

"It's strange because these dreams started before I even met you, yet somehow you were already in them."

I looked at him then, hoping he had an explanation for the dreams, needing his assurance that everything was all right.

His face was only inches from mine now and I desperately wanted to kiss him, feel his warm lips press against mine.

His voice broke my train of thought. "What do you think it means?"

"I'm not sure," I began tentatively, "but I think you should be careful. Keep your eyes open for anything unusual."

He nodded in silent agreement. "Thank you Callee."

He leaned over and gave me a quick peck on the cheek before darting back into the night.

I sat quietly for a few minutes, my hand resting over the spot where Ian had kissed me, enjoying the warmth that spread over my entire body.

The sound of approaching footsteps broke through my reverie, and I made a quick dash for the tent, silently ducking into the flap, not bothering to zip it up, worried about the sound it would make. I lay down quietly on top of my sleeping back and listened to the footsteps near my tent and pass by without even stopping.

I released the breath I was holding and got up to zip the tent door closed so no insects would come in during the night. Darkness had swallowed the world around me, but I could vaguely make out the shadowy forms of my sleeping friends in the dark and tried to avoid stepping on them While I walked.

I lay back down, knowing it would be hours before I fell asleep. Not only had a slept on a good part of the bus ride today, but also, I was afraid of having the dream again.

Eventually, I dozed off into a fitful slumber, awaking the next morning at the shuffle of feet in our tent.

The other four girls were already up and gathering their clothes and shower supplies together. I sprang up from my bed and mumbled a good morning to the girls in the tent, quickly digging in my own duffel to gather my things.

The wait for a shower was long, and we began to talk about the day's adventures while we were in line. Amber and Kathryn wanted to go to the beach and swim, but Jackie convinced them to do something else in the morning and we would all go to the beach in the afternoon to relax. "We can use Saturday to relax before going home on Sunday," she explained.

We finally decided to go hiking and agreed to meet up with the boys at breakfast to see if they wanted to come.

We reached the shower room at that moment and split up, promising to meet back at the tent before the morning meal.

I turned on the shower and let the hot water run over my aching body, knotted from spending the night on the hard ground. I tried to hurry, knowing there were still people who needed to get into the shower that morning.

I dried off and dresses in a pair of khaki shorts and a t-shirt, stepping out of the shower and over to one of the five small sinks to brush my teeth and throw my long hair into a ponytail. People were talking animatedly around me, and I smiled, enjoying the excitement coursing through the room.

Jackie had taken the sink beside mine, and I waited for her to finish so we could walk back to the tent together. There we both stashed our shower equipment, trading sandals for tennis shoes while we waited for the rest of our troupe to join us.

It wasn't hard to convince the guys to join us on our excursion, though Ian had declined the invitation, saying he had things to do today. After breakfast, we checked in with the chaperones before heading towards the hiking trail marked on our little map. We left camp at eight-thirty, which meant we only had four hours to hike before check-in at lunch, and we wasted no time in finding the trail.

Though I felt my unnatural fear of woods surface again, I quickly tampered the feeling, reassured by the presence of my friends with me.

The sun had risen overhead, promising a beautiful day. A strong breeze had picked up, tossing the pine needles into a frenzy of activity and cooling the air around us. We saw orioles and other birds flitting in the trees around us.

The morning passed quickly, and by the time we emerged from the thick woods, it was already about time for us to head back to the campsite for lunch. We laughed as we jogged along the campground, making it back only five minutes before the required time.

Ian must have been watching impatiently for our return. I saw him take a deep breath of relief when we entered the dining area. I shot him a quick look that assured him we were okay before finding a seat among the crowded campers.

After lunch, our groups headed back towards our tents to change into swimsuits for the afternoon. We said a quick goodbye to the boys before ducking into our domed living quarters, zipping the tent door closed before undressing.

I took out my own modest black two-piece, eyeing the other girl's suits with a bit of envy. Jackie looked like a swimsuit model in her yellow bikini and the other girls at least had a figure worth showing off I felt a little out of place amongst these beautiful girls, finally deciding to wear a shirt and shorts over top my swimsuit at least until we got to the beachfront.

Our campsite was only a few minutes walk from the water's edge and it did not take us long to arrive and find a place to spread our towels on the beach. I looked around, noticing several of our classmates on the shore playing volleyball and even more in the water, splashing and dunking each other under the waves.

The other girls had already lain out to tan, and I reluctantly shed my outer clothing, self-conscious of my exposed skin.

I saw several small watercrafts floating on the water and recognized the windsurfing vessels from pictures I had seen before. The boats rode along the water, seeming to drift effortlessly over the expanse. The wind pushed the sails while the riders guided the craft, and I was amazed by the grace at which the riders seemed to navigate the waters.

My gaze scanned over the water, stopping to look at each small boat. A flash of golden brown caught my attention, and I stopped to look closely at the fourth craft in from the right.

Recognition hit me almost immediately. Ian's lithe form was navigating the small vessel, running it expertly across the ocean surface.

I had always thought Ian good-looking, but the word did not seem to do him justice now. As he neared the shore, I was shocked at the muscles I saw defined across his abdomen and chest. His hair was wet, hanging in damp clumps across his forehead, which he quickly brushed aside with a sharp twist of his head.

I was not the only one caught under the powerful effect of his figure and saw many girls staring at him as he touched the shore with his small craft and even more walk up to talk with him after he returned the boat back to its owner.

Ian nodded and chatted with all of them and I could feel deep jealousy well up inside me.

As if sensing my dark mood, Ian turned head, scanning the beach, his gaze stopping immediately when our eyes met.

I hoped he couldn't see my smoldering gaze from that far away, and I ducked my head to try and hide the look marring my face.

Though I wanted to keep my head down, I risked another look at Ian, shocked to see him walking across the sand towards me, a determined expression etched on his features.

I stared at him, not able to look away from his perfect figure. His eyes flashed with an emotion I could only describe as protective, and I shivered under the intensity of his gaze.

When he finally reached where I sat I was barely holding on to my tumultuous emotions. I couldn't help but stare at the divine figure standing before me.

"Callee, may I talk to you for a moment?" There was no way for me to deny that voice, and I nodded my head in agreement.

I saw the girls look up from their spots on the sand, their eyes opening in shock when Ian flashed them with a dazzling smile. Jackie raised her eyes questioningly to mine and I sent her a reassuring look before dragging myself off the beach towel and on to my feet.

I started walking silently toward the more deserted side of the beach, my mind wondering what Ian was thinking. A warm arm slid across my back, and despite the warmth of the afternoon sun, I trembled from the intimate contact. I turned my confused eyes to Ian searching for an answer, but he kept his gaze steadily forward, refusing to look at me.

We walked that way for several minutes, the sounds of laughter fading behind us until I could no longer hear anything but the beat of my own heart. We walked almost all the way to the tree line before Ian stopped, sliding his arm from around my waist to take both hands in his.

I raised my eyes, confused by the troubled look I saw on his face.

"What's wrong Ian?"

He remained silent, his eyes never leaving my face, his thumbs absently stroking the heels of my hands.

"Ian?"

I read his turbulent emotions clearly on his face.

"Callee, I know I have no right to ask this of you, but please do not come to the beach again."

I almost laughed, but his pained gray eyes were so serious that the sound died before it ever reached my lips.

"Why?" My mind was rampant, running through a hundred possible reasons for his request.

He choked over the words of his response, his eyes burning fiercely now. "I don't want any other guys to see you in this outfit. Every time one of them looks at you, I bum with anger."

I was overwhelmed by the intensity of his expression and felt a part of me melt at his confession, yet another part of me was seething with frustration. Ian had made it clear that we were not going to be together, so what right did he have to stake any claim on me.

"Ian," I began, irritation marking my every word, "if you want me to be only yours, you can have me. I don't want apart from you, and every day it gets harder to fight my growing feelings. I know want me too. You can't ask me to be only yours if you are not going to accept my feelings."

Ian's groaned, desperately holding onto my hands as he spoke. "Callee, I want to be with you. Every inch of me begs to do what you ask, but you know why we can't be together. In the end, it will just be too painful."

"I am willing to take that risk. If getting my heart broken in the end means getting to be with you, even if just for a little while, then I am willing to take the risk." I heard the desperate edge in my voice, unable to hold it back now. "Ian, I love you. When the time comes for you to go, I will not ask you to stay, but for now, I want to be with you."

I stood on my tiptoes and placed my hands on Ian's hard chest, powerless to resist the desire inside me any longer. My lips pressed against Ian's and I tried to transfer my thoughts to him through the soft kiss.

A moan escaped Ian's throat moments before I felt his hand touch my cheek, silently urging the kiss deeper. Nothing else mattered at that moment and the world around me fell away until only Ian and myself existed.

I don't know how long the kiss went on, but I was panting by the time Ian finally lifted his lips from mine.

He closed his eyes, pressing his forehead to mine as we both caught our breath.

"Are you sure this is what you want, Callee?"

The whispered words buoyed my heart and I leaned in to answer his question with another searing kiss.

Soft footsteps behind me made me turn, and I saw Jackie slowly approaching us with an apologetic look on her face.

"I'm sorry to interrupt, but we have to check-in. It's time for supper." She spoke the words with a smile, then turned to leave us alone again. I had to remember to thank her later.

I looked into Ian's eyes again, seeing the mixed emotions still in his silver eyes.

"It will be okay Ian. This is what I want," I assured him.

He looked at me intently for a few minutes, and for the first time since we left the beach, I saw a deep smile form on his lips.

"Callee, there is something I have been wanting to show you, but it will have to be at night. Do you think you can get away from your tent again and meet me right here tomorrow night after dark?"

I nodded as I turned pulling him with me so we could collect our things from the beach before going back for supper.

My heart had taken flight, and I smiled happily, hardly believing this was real, as Ian and I walked hand in hand down the sandy shore.

~ 13 ~

"So, tell me again what happened?"

Jackie had been steadily asking me this question ever since she saw Ian and I kissing on the beach, and every time I told the story the truth became a little more real to me.

Now, lying in the darkened tent, I had finally come to terms with the reality of what had happened this afternoon.

I couldn't keep the smile off my face as I again recounted every detail I could remember, withholding only the information that might leak Ian's secret.

The other girls were all listening intently. Even in the almost pitch black, I could feel their eyes upon me as I spoke.

"It's still unreal," I said after I had finished. It was like my whole world had come alive, ecstasy filling every corner of my mind, radiating outward to the rest of my body. My life before now had been lifeless and dull. Now, vivid colors lit my world.

After an hour of questioning, my friends finally drifted off to sleep, leaving me to think about the rest of the conversation Ian and I had at the beach. I wasn't sure what he wanted to show me tomorrow night, but I could hardly wait for the time to be alone with Ian again.

The next morning passed just like the previous. We got up and showered before heading to breakfast, where we met up with the boys. Ian surprised me by taking the seat next to mine and eating breakfast with me, talking easily with my friends as if he had always known them. I saw Nathan glower from across the table, but I wasn't going to let anything dampen my mood.

Once again Ian refused my invitation to go hiking, and I nodded in understanding. I could read the gratitude in his molten eyes before he leaned down to give me a scintillating kiss. I knew my friends had stopped eating their breakfast and were now gaping openmouthed at the public show of affection, but I didn't care if everyone knew howl felt about Ian. I.

When the kiss ended and I was once again aware of our surroundings, I was shocked to realize that not only had my friends been watching, but almost all the students present were looking in our direction, stunned by the apparently new relationship.

I blushed furiously but tried to remind myself that I had no reason to be embarrassed. Determined to act nonchalant, I picked up my fork and speared a bite of egg off my plate, chewing and swallowing methodically before picking up another piece.

By the third bite, I could still feel the stares from all around me. I quickly excused myself, feigning an excuse about leaving something in the tent.

I flashed Ian a quick smile as I picked up my tray, dumping it in a trashcan as I practically ran out of the small enclosure.

I raced back to the tent and just sat until I was once again my normal tan color.

I caught up with my friends at the edge of the campground as they were checking in with the chaperone for the morning. Nobody paid much attention to my return except Nathan, who was openly glaring at me.

I swallowed hard at the betrayed expression he wore, promising myself that I would talk to him and clear everything up the first chance I got.

Luckily, that opportunity presented itself quickly. We had just entered the marshy trail that was to be our hike for the day when Nathan put his hand on my arm, holding me back while the rest of the group plowed on ahead.

"Why didn't you tell me you were with Evans?" Nathan started coolly, his eyes never leaving the trail in front of him.

"I'm sorry Nathan. Honestly, it just happened yesterday and it was so. . .unexpected. I never really had time to process it let alone tell anybody. Jackie was the only one who knew because she walked in on the moment"

I was looking at him, but Nathan never turned in my direction, instead, he walked silently along the worn path.

"Nathan, I swear I would have told you."

Nothing.

I started to panic. I knew Nathan had liked me, but could it have gone even deeper than that?

I didn't know when we had stopped walking, but the world around us was still now, only the soft swaying of the trees moving around us.

"Nathan, please say something."

"Do you really like him Callee?" Nathan looked at me then, ready to read every look that crossed my face.

I thought about Ian's silvery-gray eyes, -his warmth, the way I felt when he kissed me.

"Yes, I really like him," I answered, barely above a whisper.

Nathan's gaze stayed on me, assessing the truth of my words. Finally, he nodded, a resigned look on his face. He started walking again, and I took a couple of quick steps to catch up.

"After you left breakfast today I took Ian aside to talk to him alone."

My face must have been horribly twisted because a smile lit Nathan's lips."

"Don't worry Callee, I didn't beat him up or anything. I just warned him that he better treats you right or he will have to answer to me."

I didn't even think as I lunged at Nathan, wrapping him in a tight hug, trying to display all the emotions I was feeling in that one embrace. Nathan wrapped his arms around me, returning the hug gently.

"I love you Callee. I don't care if Ian is your boyfriend now, I will always be there if you need me." The words were spoken earnestly, and I knew he meant everyone.

"Thanks, Nathan," I finally said, surprised to find tears in my eyes. No matter what happened with Ian, I knew I would always be able to count on Nathan to be there for me.

We had to jog after that to catch up to the group, but Nathan deftly held onto my hand to keep me from tripping over the bumpy path as we went.

I was anxious for the day to end so I could slip off to the beach and see Ian, but my impatience only made the time crawl slower. Every five minutes I found myself glancing at my watch only to be disappointed by the small increment of time that had actually passed.

What could he possibly want to show me?

That thought had been -circulating in my head the entire morning. By the time, we finally hit the beach to relax for the evening, I was so would up I felt that I would jump out of my skin.

I scanned the beach, desperately searching for Ian's familiar figure among the crowd, only to be met by his apparent absence.

Per Ian's request, I kept my tank top and shorts on today while we lay out on the sandy beachfront. I tried to relax but to no avail. Finally, after fifteen minutes of fidgeting, I gave up and convinced Kathryn to walk with me along the beach.

The waves lapped at our feet as we walked, and I let the cool water soothe my soles, tired from the past two days' hikes. I was grateful for Kathryn's company and she kept up a steady stream of chatter, thoroughly distracting me from my previous train of thought.

At supper, Ian once again sat with us to eat, his presence reawakening my earlier curiosity. I knew I was quiet during the meal, and several times Jackie asked if I was feeling okay. I assured her I felt fine before lapsing into silence again.

People slowly began breaking off into groups for the evening, some playing cards, the boys once again picking up the football for a short game. Ian was on the sidelines watching as the guys divided up into teams and began playing. I watched Ian from the shelter house, never taking my eyes off him.

I was surprised when he walked onto the field and whispered something in one of the guys' ears. The kid smiled then gestured to the rest of the team, and I realized Ian must have been asking permission to join the game.

I watched with interest as he ran with the football, gracefully dodging several outstretched hands, effortlessly crossing into the end zone almost every time he carried the ball. Most of the students had stopped their individual activities to watch the game as it coach continued.

It was hard to believe that Ian knew the secrets of the universe, yet here he was intensely enjoying a simple game of touch football.

The time passed quickly and I jumped when the teacher standing behind yelled for everybody to return to their tents for the night.

Ian took several congratulatory pats on the back and invites to join next year's football team as he made his way back to where I now stood. His eyes were dancing with excitement as he gently lifted my hand to his mouth, caressing it with a soft kiss.

"Tonight, after dark." Those smooth words were enough to send shivers down my spine, and I nodded my head mutely in agreement.

Ian glided off in the direction of his tent without another word, leaving me standing at the picnic table still shaking from his kiss.

The girls practically had to guide me back to the tent. As we entered the flap to our dwelling, I told them about my late-night rendezvous, begging them to understand and to keep my absence a secret from everybody. They had agreed almost immediately with my assurance that I would give them details of the meeting tomorrow on the bus ride home.

I dressed in black sweatpants and a black t-shirt, praying it would be enough to disguise my escape from our campsite. There was nothing left to do now except wait, and I sat down on my sleeping bag, rocking back and forth impatiently while the light completely faded from the sky around our sleeping quarters.

When it was completely dark out, I quietly undid the tent flap and crept out into the night, zipping the door closed again behind me. I listened to the night around me, straining to hear beyond the chirping of crickets and other insects for any signs of danger. When I was sure the coast was clear, I began to move, stooping low to hide in the shadows of tents that I passed, trying to keep my footsteps light. The slight crunch of grass and the steady pounding of my heart were the only things I heard as I made my way through camp towards the beach.

I didn't see anybody on my trip and soon I was running along the sandy shore, dimly lit by the moon overhead, searching for the spot where Ian had asked me to meet him.

I saw him before anything else, his faint glow ushering me closer to the spot where he waited. I slowed, allowing my heart to calm down as I approached him. I could see his smile widen as I got closer, and I reached out, taking his hand as I stopped where he stood.

"Callee." His velvety voice drifted along the breeze coming off the bay, and I smiled contentedly at the delight coursing through my veins. "This is something I have wanted to show you for a long time."

He lifted me into his arms effortlessly, and I immediately cuddled in to rest my head on his chest. The warmth radiated off his body, and I breathed in his sweet, irresistible scent.

"Are you ready?"

I nodded my head as I looked steadily into his may eyes. He smiled tenderly, and the next thing I knew, we were in the air.

I gasped in surprise at the sudden change in altitude but found that I wasn't afraid. Ian is arms supported me and I felt safe there, cradled next to his hard body.

He waited for me to adjust to the height, then slowly leaned forward, pushing us out overtop the bay. I turned my head to look down at the water and gasped in delight.

The moon glimmered off the small waves cresting below us, its wavering reflection dancing on the water's surface. I extended my view, glancing out across the bay at the endless expanse of water.

Ian glanced down, taking in the look on my face and smiling at the joy he saw reflected there.

He turned slightly, angling us back to shore. We briefly floated over the sand before it gave way to the lush pine forest. I was once again in awe as I watched thousands of trees swaying to the beat of the wind.

I gave a slight gasp as Ian plunged into the midst of the woods, swerving to avoid the trees in front of us. He was moving so fast now I could hardly see any detail in the faint light, the world around me dimming to a dark green blur.

It didn't take long for us to emerge on the other side of the woods, and Ian slowed, touching back down to the ground and setting me on my feet.

"Ian, that was incredible." I couldn't keep the awe from showing in my voice.

"I have always thought so," he said, cradling my cheek in his palm, "but I have never enjoyed it more than I did tonight."

His eager lips touched mine in a deep, intense kiss, and I responded with the same fervor. It was several minutes before we broke away from each other, and I heard his labored breathing against my cheek and felt the rapid rise and fall of his chest beneath my palms.

"Callee, I have so much I want to tell you, so much I want to show you, but when we are together, I can think about nothing except you — your sweet voice, your warm heart, the softness of your skin. You drown every one of my senses. It takes all my willpower to keep from sweeping you away, to remember why I am here."

His confession stole my breath away and I was lost in his dusky eyes.

"Ian, I love you. It's impossible for me to remember my life before you came into it."

"I love you too, Callee. No matter what, I hope you know that."

We kissed again, our entwined figures bathed in the moonlight. I don't know how long we stood like that, but all too soon Ian disentangled himself from me.

"We need to get back to camp. I think we both need some sleep tonight," he said with a regretful smile.

I checked my watch, stunned to see that it was almost four in the morning.

Ian gave me one last kiss before picking me up again in his arms.

This time I was not surprised when we lifted into the air and settled into his embrace for the journey back to the other side of the woods.

~ 14 ~

I heard Ian knocking on the front door and grabbed my last piece of toast, slinging my book bag across my back as I ran to greet him.

We had been back from fall break for a little over a week and ever since then Ian had come to walk me to school each morning. I had insisted we still stop and pick Nathan up on our way, and it had become the new tradition for the three of us to walk to school together.

The first morning when he had shown up at our front door, my parents had been waiting in the living room, and I smile apologetically at Ian as I dragged him in to meet them.

Ian had been perfect, flawlessly introducing himself and answering each of my parent's questions, and I could tell by their warm smiles that my mother and father both approved of the boy I was dating. After ten minutes I had finally put an end to the inquisition insisting Ian and I needed to leave for school.

"Good morning beautiful," he greeted me, his gray eyes grazing over my face before pulling me in for a kiss.

It no longer made me blush when Ian kissed me in public, and I matched his enthusiasm with my own lips. As usual, I forgot the time, fully focused on the moment.

Finally, Ian pulled away from me, tucking my hair behind my ear with his free hand. He smiled warmly. "We better start walking or I will start kissing you again and we will most definitely be late."

A sudden rumbling in the distance made me break his gaze, and I noticed the sky to the west was dark, covered in storm clouds that would surely reach West Liberty by mid-morning.

"Looks like we are in for some bad weather," I said offhandedly.

Ian followed my gaze, frowning at the approaching storm. He focused intently on the threatening clouds, his frown deepening as he took in the blackened sky. Something about the look in his eyes made me shudder with fear.

"Ian?" I touched his face lightly and his eyes flashed back to mine, the apprehensive look leaving his face as he took in my frightened expression.

He gave me another smile, though I thought it looked a little less genuine than before, and took my hand, leading me down the sidewalk towards

Nathan's house. Nathan's steady chatter filled the silence that morning, and I tried to pay attention to what he was saying, but my mind was distracted by Ian's reaction to the approaching storm.

He was quiet still, not contributing anything to the conversation and I couldn't help but think that something was wrong. It was strange that Ian was so affected by the dark clouds, and I had never seen him react this way to a simple thunderstorm before.

The unease stayed with me all morning, and I kept glancing at Ian during our first and second-period classes, trying to read the concerned expression on his face.

The thunder was approaching, its boom shaking the walls of the small school and resounding deep within my chest. Every time it rumbled, Ian jumped, his nervousness seeming to grow exponentially with each crash.

The rain finally came, driving hard against the walls of the school. I watched it conic down in torrents, creating a sheet of water on the school windows. The world outside was completely gray, the trees and houses looking ashen under the cloud cover.

It was lunchtime before I finally pulled Ian aside and demanded he tell me what was causing his panic.

"Something just doesn't feel right. I don't know what it is, but it feels. . .dark."

I looked at him, feeling his words sink deep into my body, creating a sense of dread that far surpassed my earlier unease. My dream from the bus was suddenly forefront in my mind, and I clung desperately to Ian's hand as I looked around the crowded cafeteria, trying to assess any peril that may be hiding there.

The cafeteria was brightly lit and student voices created a roaring din in the room. Nothing unusual was happening and I relaxed a little, feeling no threat in the room.

I turned back to Ian, who had also been studying his surroundings.

"I don't sense anything here," he said, confirming my earlier appraisal, "but I can't help but feel that something is coming. Something dangerous."

He was looking at me now, his eyes full of concern. "Callee, if something happens, if anything seems out of place, I want you to get out of here. Run, make up an excuse to leave, and go home immediately."

His hands were trembling as he cupped my cheek, and his obvious fear only increased my own.

"What about you?" I finally managed to choke out. I knew that if Ian was in danger, there is no way I would leave.

"I will be fine," he promised, leaning down to seal the vow with a soft kiss.

I could only stare at him mutely as the bell rang and students began dutifully heading to class.

Luckily the next period was study hall, which required nothing of me, allowing my mind to wander where it wished.

I was on the edge of my seat, waiting for something to happen, but the class ended uneventfully and I caught up with Ian, slipping my hand into his while we walked to chemistry.

Nothing was out of the ordinary, and class was continuing as usual. Suddenly a loud crack of lightning lit the sky, and the lights in the classroom flickered before going dead, washing the room in blackness.

I could hear the surprised screams of several girls in the class, but I did not scream. I was on my feet immediately, surprised to find Ian already beside me.

"Get out of here," he whispered fiercely in my ear.

I turned my head, caught off guard by the urgency in his voice.

"Nobody panic." The calm tone of our teacher broke through the excited din of student voices. "Lightening probably just hit the school, knocking out power. Hopefully, the generator will kick on in a few minutes and we will continue class. Everybody remain in your seats."

I stared at the place where I knew Ian stood. "Ian, I'm sure it was just the lightning. Everything is fine."

The lights kicked back on, eliciting a groan from the students in the class. I saw the wild look in Ian's eyes then, and I tried desperately to think of a way to reassure him.

"Please take your seat, Mr. Evans." The order was delivered sternly from the front of the room, and I gave Ian a little nudge to send him back in that direction, smiling in what I hoped was an encouraging look.

He didn't take his eyes off me, stalling in the middle of the aisle to stare at my face.

"Mr. Evans!"

Ian sent me one last nervous glance before turning and walking the short distance to his desk.

The class continued as if the blackout had never happened, but I knew it was still bothering Ian, who kept his gaze permanently fixated on where I sat.

When the bell rang, Ian practically leaped out of his seat and was at my side immediately.

He walked with me to history, all the while shooting glances around the crammed hallway.

We were at the door and I was about to walk across the threshold when his hand pulled on my arm, bringing me back into the hallway.

His eyes were staring into mine when he spoke. "Callee, I need to run to my locker and get my history homework. Jenkins will give me a detention for sure if I don't have it. I will be back."

His eyes, the color of the storm outside, locked with mine and I could see a hundred emotions in their hazy depths as he bent his head to give me an urgent kiss.

Without another word, he turned and quickly wove his way through the mass of students, leaving me standing at the door in stunned silence. I wanted to run after him, but the crowd of students behind me carried me into the history room.

I took my seat, and my eyes automatically went to the door to watch for Ian's return. In the back of my mind, I knew he wasn't coming back, but I sat praying fervently that I was wrong.

When the bell rang, my suspicion was confirmed and I rose out of my seat, prepared to leave the classroom.

"Miss Edwards, sit down. Class has started."

Mr. Jenkins's commanding voice permeated the quiet room, and I looked at him with all the loathing I could muster.

"I need to go to the bathroom," I stated firmly, not backing away from Mr. Jenkins's demand.

He smiled cruelly. "I heard about the time you disappeared from study hall with that excuse. It will not work with me. Sit down immediately."

The students were staring at me, their eyes opened in shock at the scene unfolding before them.

"Miss Edwards, if you do not take your seat, I will see to it that you are suspended from the school for insubordination."

If I was suspended from school, I would surely be grounded for the next several months, which meant never seeing Ian or anybody else outside of class.

My shaky legs buckled under me, and I sat down defeated in my seat. MI. Jenkins just smiled victoriously as he began his lesson for the day.

I waited impatiently for the time to pass, my frustration and worry growing with every second that ticked by.

Where could Ian have gone? And why didn't he tell me he was leaving?

I felt trapped in the small classroom. It was like invisible chains had bound my body to the desk, and no matter how I struggled, I could not break flee from their grasp.

I began to hyperventilate, my breathing nothing more than small gasps of air. What if something happened to Ian? He had said that he felt an ominous presence, and my dream had surely indicated that something evil was coming after him.

Where had Ian gone?

That question plagued me the most. He could have easily left West Liberty.

NO! I wouldn't let myself think that. He said he couldn't leave until he was called, so he must be here somewhere. I wracked my brain, trying hard to ebb the panic there to think straight. Inside my mind, something finally clicked. There was only one place he would go.

The bell rang and I vaulted from my seat, out the door before anybody else had their bags packed. I didn't even bother to go to my locker but ran down the hall and out the front door into the pouring rain. I didn't even stop on the sidewalk, but turned toward the city park and broke into a sprint.

The rain-soaked my hair and clothes, weighing me down as I ran, and the wind was blowing hard against my face, but I didn't stop or slow my run. The buildings around me slipped by un-noticed. I wasn't paying attention to anything except getting to Ian.

Lightening was still striking in the distance, its brilliant flash lighting the sky moments before a roll of thunder shook the ground.

I reached the city park and plunged down the path, the fear I usually felt overridden by my need to get to Ian.

The pathway was even darker than normal, and the trees that normally blocked the gusting wind couldn't hold back the strong air stream now.

I was still running, my lungs begging for air as I stumbled along the dirt path.

Why was it taking so long to get there? I had never run so hard in my life, but still, it felt like ages since I'd left school.

Finally, I saw the clearing up ahead that marked the begin-ning of the swinging bridge and I felt a moment of relief.

I burst into the clearing, stopping at last and bending over to inhale deeply. My head came up and I looked around me, search-ing the area for any sign of Ian.

There was nobody on the bridge or in the clearing, and I felt my hopes plummet. Still, I was not ready to give up and took several steps forward until I was standing on the bridge, extending my field of vision.

A brilliant flash of lightning forced me to look up at the sky overhead, and I felt my breathing stop.

Ian was looking down at me from the air, a look of sheer panic in his gray eyes as he took in my figure on the bridge. I felt relief mingled with fear as I realized he wasn't alone, and I turned my head to get a better look at the other person in the sky.

She was beautiful, and my breath caught as I looked at her. She was a few inches taller than me, with porcelain skin glowing against the black of her t-shirt and pants, which were form fitting against the slim curves of her body. Her long blonde hair was pulled back into a tight ponytail, clearly revealing her high cheekbones and well-shaped mouth. Despite this, it was something else entirely that held me still on the bridge below.

An eerie smile curved on her lips as she looked at me with bright, violet eyes.

"Well, well." Her voice was the same beautiful honey-tone as Ian's, but it did not hold the warmth that his hand. Instead, it was cold as ice, sending shivers down my spine.

I instinctively took a step backward as she floated down, landing gracefully on the bridge only a few feet away from me.

"Who do we have here?" she said, her sinister smile growing wider as she took another step towards me.

~ 15 ~

"Callee, get out of here." Ian issued the command, his voice shaking with panic and terror.

"Callee, huh," the creature in front of me purred, taking another step in my direction. "What a lovely name. Tell me Callee, what are you doing here in the middle of the woods during such a storm."

Ian swooped down from the sky and landed on the bridge, placing his body directly between the girls and mine.

"Leave her alone. She has nothing to do with this," Ian said, his voice harsh as he spoke to the girl in front of me.

The girl's petrifying smile widened another fraction of an inch, her violet eyes flashing with interest. "This girl means a great deal to you, doesn't she?"

"Ian, who is she?" I tried to keep my fear from leaking into the question, but to- no avail.

Ian didn't look at me as he answered. "She is one of the fallen." His tone was icy as he spoke the words.

I felt my heartbeat double, sensing the danger his tone conveyed.

"What does she want?" I could barely choke the words out.

His jaw tensed and I could barely understand the words he ground out from behind clenched teeth. "She wants me to become one of them."

"Why you?" I could not believe the scene unfolding before me.

"Fallen angels have made a dark pact, part of which grants them knowledge which is unknown to angels of the common order. It is one of the tools which is used to convince angels of heaven to join the fallen. There is something about me that she knows, something she thinks the dark ones can use in their struggle with the forces of good." He said the words like they were poison in his mouth.

Anger, strong as anything I had ever felt before, welled up inside of me. I stepped to the side, just enough so I could see the girl from around Ian's broad shoulders. "He will never join yon," I hissed at her. "You are full of wickedness and deceit. Ian is nothing like you."

I don't know what I meant to accomplish by my words, but it did not seem to have any effect on the dark figure before me.

The wind was blowing in full force in the clearing, making the bridge rock dangerously back and forth and I had to grab onto the railing to keep myself steady as I spoke the words. Neither Ian nor the girl seemed the least bit affected by the bridges swaying.

"You think it is all bad, but you are wrong," the girl said, her eyes deadest on Ian and me. "I am free to go where I want when I want. I do not have to answer to anybody else. Surely you can think of a benefit that this freedom brings me, that it would bring to you if you were to join me."

As much as I wanted to deny her words, I couldn't help but imagine Ian always by my side, never being tormented by our relationship, and never having to leave West Liberty.

I glanced up at Ian and knew he was thinking the same thing. His eyes were tom, as he looked back at me longingly.

Ian had warned me before that getting involved with me would make him a risk even to himself, but it had not crossed my mind how our love could be used against him. Yet I had made a promise that I would never make him choose me. As hard as it was to wish otherwise, Ian needed my encouragement now.

"Nothing you can say will ever make him turn. You are wasting your breath with this ranting."

I forced myself to say the words, and it cost me dearly to utter them out loud. It only made it more obvious that Ian and I would not have a forever, yet there was no way I would ever be able to let him turn from the Ian I loved into one of these dark creatures.

I saw Ian straighten, his eyes once again taking on the defiant fight I had seen before. I knew we would have to present a united front, one that would remain unshakable even under the treachery of the dark angel, so I too stood taller, glaring at the girl across from me.

The girl before me was glaring with outright contempt at us now, but she quickly masked the expression with one of disregard.

"Very well then." Her voice sounded bored, but I could see the excitement rising in her eyes. "If you will not turn, I will just have to destroy you."

Before I even registered a movement, she had spanned the distance between us, slamming into Ian with an impact that sent them both plummeting over the side of the bridge.

"Ian" The terrified words tore from my throat as I rushed to look over the railing at where they had disappeared.

I heard the sound of air moving behind me, and turned just in time to see Ian fly up on the other side of the bridge, a black streak following closely behind him.

I watched in horror as Ian turned to meet the oncoming figure. Lightening flashed, lighting the air in time for me to see the dark streak run into Ian with the speed of an oncoming train.

I screamed, sure that it would knock him out of the air, but he had expertly grabbed hold of her arms and kicked his legs, flipping her harmlessly over top of his body. She spun out of control for a second but quickly regained her orientation, kicking off a nearby tree to make another attack.

The fight seemed to go on endlessly as I watched helplessly on the rocking bridge. Every time the dark angel attacked, Ian would redirect the assault or dodge it, escaping unharmed each time.

A strange mixture of fear and awestruck embraced me as I watched his smooth, fluid movements in the air. It was like an intricate dance, graceful, and terrifying all at once.

The girl made another pass at Ian, and he once again pushed her effortlessly aside, sending her careening into the bridge. She hit the wooden planks with a thud, jarring the suspension bridge and forcing me to tighten my grasp on the rope to which I'd been clinging.

She lay there, not moving as the rain beat against her crumpled form. Ian stayed suspended in mid-air readying himself against another physical assault. I could recall every detail about his appearance, his silvery eyes, his blonde hair, letting it fill my vision one last time.

The body on the bridge raised herself slowly, finally standing despite the obvious pain she was in.

"I will make you suffer." She spat the words at Ian, anger, and hatred dripping from every syllable.

Before I could move, the dark figure was behind me, one arm wrapped around my neck and the other holding my hands helplessly behind my back. I could feel her cut off my airway.

"Callee." The words tore from Ian's throat as he landed on the bridge, only feet away from me. "Let her go." The pain in his eyes made me want to reach out and hold him, but despite my insistent struggling, I was unable to move from the tight gasp enfolding me.

His eyes were wild, desperate, and I felt his fear from where I stood. I knew I was going to die, I wanted desperately to tell him I loved him one last time, but I could not say the words.

My vision was becoming spotty, and I knew the lack of oxygen was beginning to affect me. I took in Ian's appearance, his silvery eyes, his blonde hair, every other detail I could recall about him, letting it fill my vision one last time.

I love you. The words formed on my mind and I willed him to feel what I could not say.

This is it, I thought desperately, as I prepared myself for the end.

~ 16 ~

"Callee...Callee, wake up."

I fluttered my eyelids a couple of times adjusting my vision to the newly radiant light that was pouring through my pupils. I felt like a baby who had just been born and was seeing the world for the first time.

I looked around the room, wait I take that back, rooms I was in. Every room was in a continuous loop of merging and dividing walls, doors, and the occasional chair. I felt like I was watching a petri dish culture that was constantly changing.

How could this be happening? How could I be standing here? Wait, where is here? A voice. I definitely remember hearing a voice.

"So, I see you are finally awake," said a voice inside my head. "Lovely of you to join us, Cal. Can I call you Cal?"

I looked around trying to figure out where the voice was coming from.

"I'm sure you have lots of questions. There will be plenty of time for that later." I continued searching for the voice. It sounded very familiar like I had heard it somewhere before. "I don't have very long with you, so I must make this quick."

I then realized why I had recognized the familiar voice, it was my voice. I was speaking to myself. Only I wasn't the one in control of what I was saying.

I heard my voice again, "Callee, did you hear what I said? I need to send you back, Ian needs you."

Ian. That name sent every memory from the past couple of weeks back into my brain. I remembered the dance, the sweet smell of his skin, and his warm touch. I remember his kiss. I longed to taste his lips again.

But, where was Ian? Why wasn't he here with me now? I remembered, another angel. One of the fallen. She was keeping me away from Ian. She was trying to take away everything that I had dreamed of.

I wasn't going to let her take Ian away from me. I was angry. I was beyond angry I was furious. I could feel my blood burning on my insides. My face was getting hot. The knuckles on my hands were white from clenching my fists so tight.

The pseudo-voice inside my head continued to coach me from my own lips. Only now my voice sounded harsher. "Yes, she is the one who is to blame. We must destroy her."

As the coaching and anger continued to grow they like the rooms around me started merging until the voice was no longer that of someone else's, but it was my own. Rage and hatred rushed over me as my body started to shake uncontrollably.

The rooms surrounding me began to close in. I couldn't breathe. As if the walls were trying to suffocate me, trying to keep me from him. As the rooms created my own personal coffin, I rolled all of my emotions together, and let out one final scream.

I woke up to the same warm hands I was used to. Ian had my face pressed against his chest. "Callee are you ok?"

I lifted my head to gaze at Ian, he looked as if he had been through a war. His shirt was ripped in enough places that it's a wonder it even stayed on his body.

I opened my mouth half expecting the words that came out to not be my own. However, after I forced the air to and from my lungs a couple of times. I asked him

"Where is she?"

Looking at me with a shocked expression Ian answered. "You don't remember what happened?" I pathetically shook my head from side to side. "After you lost consciousness, I thought I had lost you for good. The fallen angel let you go and I slammed into her as hard as I could. We fought back and forth for a while, neither one gaining the advantage."

I looked up at him again and he continued.

"As we were fighting a big bolt of sapphire lightning struck right where you lay. I thought you to be dead for sure, but to my surprise, you stood right up from where you lay. The fallen one charged right after you, but you started hurling blue lightning bolts over and over again at her until it was too much for her to handle. She fled into the woods to the north."

After hearing Ian's recollection of the events that just occurred every bone in my body wanted to go after her and finish what I had started with the lightning, but when I looked at Ian, the bewilderment on his face was concerning.

He bent down to me. I could smell the fragrance of honeysuckle as he kissed me on the cheek.

On his way, back he stopped by my ear, his breath was warm on my naked lobe. He whispered just audible enough for me to hear. "Callee, I'm so glad that you are safe, but I need to know something and it could be the difference between losing West Liberty and saving it."

I looked at him one more time, almost scared of what he was going to ask and the impact it would have on my family, my friends, my town, and those important to me like Ian. Ian's chest and arms tightened around me as he asked. "Who are you and what have you done with Callee?"

A shower of blue lightning surrounded myself and Ian. It sent him flying through the sky and into a large tree on the other side of the bridge. The tree cracked and fell to the ground. I tried to run to him but my body wouldn't move.

I felt my legs start to support me as I stood and casually strolled over to Ian's body. I stared at him through my new sapphire blue eyes as the corners of my mouth turn up into a grin.

I tried to get myself to stop but my mouth cracked open and the wannabe-voice from before answered Ian's question.

"You may call me the Dark Prince."

www.ingramcontent.com/pod-product-compliance
Lightning Source LLC
Chambersburg PA
CBHW071834190726

48292CB00005B/1777